THREE FIRES

DENISE MINA is the *New York Times* bestselling author of *The End of the Wasp Season* and *Gods and Beasts*. Her recent novel *Conviction* was chosen as a Reese's Book Club pick. *Rizzio* is her latest novella published by Pegasus Crime. She is a regular contributor on the subject of crime fiction for television and radio. Denise lives in Glasgow, Scotland.

THREE FIRES

DENISE
MINA

PEGASUS CRIME
NEW YORK LONDON

THREE FIRES

Pegasus Crime is an imprint of
Pegasus Books, Ltd.
148 West 37th Street, 13th Floor
New York, NY 10018

First Pegasus Books cloth edition August 2023

ISBN: 978-1-63936-455-8

10 9 8 7 6 5 4 3 2 1

Printed in the United States of America
Distributed by Simon & Schuster
www.pegasusbooks.com

In his *Fire Sermon* the Buddha identified three poisons or three fires, the negative qualities of mind that cause all of the world's problems: greed, hatred and delusion.

'. . . the temper of the multitude is fickle. While it is easy to persuade them of a thing, it is hard to fix them in that persuasion . . . in our own days the Friar Girolamo Savonarola had not the means to keep those who had been believers steadfast or to make unbelievers believe.'

Machiavelli, *The Prince*

THE CONFESSION

The Great Hall, Palazzo della Signoria
Florence, Wednesday 18 April 1498

It's late afternoon as Fra Girolamo Savonarola shuffles onto the raised stage at the front of the Hall of the Five Hundred. He drags his sandalled feet, scuffing the stone floor with a *shush, shush, shush*.

Savonarola commissioned this chamber, currently the largest room in Europe. It was built to hold the five-hundred-strong Grand Council, part of the new Republic of Florence established under his authority. The vast walls are plain, not yet frescoed. Through the high windows a clear spring light floods into the room from the west.

The full council watch him walk on in silence. They are seated in neat rows, but standing behind them and around them are a substantial portion of the male population of Florence. Everyone is perfectly still and listening. It hasn't rained in Florence for a week and the men have walked dust from the street into the room. It floats above them like a scum on a broth, swimming in the warm air, rising high.

Savonarola looks out at the gathered crowd and admits that God is not talking to him. He made it up.

He has been lying to them for years.

He admits that his prophecies were so accurate because he knew certain things in advance: anyone could see that Lorenzo de' Medici was desperately ill, that Pope Innocent VIII was obese and spectacularly debauched, that the King of Naples was very old. Accurately predicting their deaths was a cheap trick that he did to get power for himself. He didn't foresee the French Army invading Brescia six years before war was even declared, he just got lucky. He didn't foretell the coming of plague, famine and war to Florence. It was a coincidence that those things happened years after he said they would.

There is no mention of the Charles the Affable prophecy because that's impossible to explain.

The shocking announcement reverberates around the room, echoes over the heads of the gathered crowd. Some of them are here because they couldn't believe he was actually going to do this. They still cherish their belief in him, have given up so much for him; they needed to hear it themselves to really take it in. Others have always known he was a fraud and a liar and have been waiting years for him to own up. But even among them the mood isn't triumphant. Even they feel something die.

Savonarola hangs his head and sags with shame.

He is not speaking these words himself. They're being read out by one of his inquisitors from his confession, extracted under torture, written down by a scribe and signed by him. But he's standing there and he's not disputing it.

A fellow Dominican, Fra Domenico, was arrested with him and subjected to even more intense torture, but Domenico isn't in the hall confessing in front of everyone. He held fast: he still ecstatically and completely believes Savonarola was chosen and directed by God. But it's not a fair comparison because they are being asked different questions: Domenico is being asked if he still has faith in Savonarola. Savonarola is being asked if he still believes in himself.

Savonarola stands as the full confession is read in a loud braying baritone, his head slumping forward on his weak neck. His nose looks bigger because his face is drawn. His shoulders are small and sloped. They've all heard him speak: he's a famous preacher. They're familiar with the rhythms and cadences of his voice and know that the document doesn't sound like him. But it's signed by him and he's there, in front of them, owning it. There's no doubt it is his.

I lied.
I am no prophet.
I have not received messages from God.
I said these things to get power.
I lied to you.

I was vainglorious.
I was informed of sundry illnesses and so could foretell the
deaths of certain powerful men.
I was told the French were coming.
I lied to you all.

Four pages of this. Four pages. At the end of the reading
he is asked by officials if it is his own true confession.

He nods.

Not good enough. Say it.

It is my own true confession, he says.

Louder, for the people at the back of the room.

IT IS MY OWN TRUE CONFESSION.

His voice clatters to the high ceiling. It resonates
from bare wall to bare wall until it dies away and is just
a memory.

A pause.

Savonarola hears air sucked slowly in through
teeth, sniffs, affirming grunts, despairing sighs. A
Sniveller, one of his loyalists, sobs quietly at the back
of the room. Savonarola's life is nothing but fractured
fragments, connected, somehow. Bits of moments.
This moment.

His withered arms are bound behind his back. His
knees are swollen. Everything hurts. He looks up to
the high windows and the light, at the dust motes
swimming aimlessly in the warm air above their heads,
and imagines that each speck is an iota of faith leaving
a person in the room.

He is a preacher. His life's mission is to bring people to God, to faith.

He didn't think anything else could hurt him, but this blow lands so deep that it takes him back thirty years, to Ferrara and Laodamia Strozzi.

AN INCEL MISHEARING

Ferrara 1470

What a wonderful thing is love. What a glorious, febrile thing is young love. Immoderate and wild, uncontained and uncontainable, fathoms of thick cream that can be curdled in an instant by a single acid drop.

Laodamia Strozzi moves like a mist. Her skin is the colour of milk. She glides on tiny slippered feet through a landscape of marbled columns and red frescos.

Girolamo Savonarola is a brilliant young man. That's the consensus in the family. Born third of seven children, he's the stand-out, and today his glorious adult life begins: he has chosen her for his wife. He has come here to formally propose.

Girolamo is skinny and confident with a bright future and a magnificent Roman nose. He's wearing his best suit of clothes: brown velvet, neat with very little adornment. He wants to look adult and serious. They'll talk about this day for the rest of their lives and it's important that he gets it right. He hates all these ribbons and velvets and fur trims that everyone is wearing these days. He's a serious person.

He steps up from the dusty street and knocks at the huge door. His breathing is shallow. There is an outbreak of plague in the poorer parts of the city, but he knows his hands are only sweating with excitement. He feels fine otherwise.

It is a warm day. The sun hits the front of the villa, and a breeze whips up dust from the street. Carts pass along the street behind him; the morning market is breaking up a couple of streets away, outside the ducal palazzo.

He lives in the villa next door to Laodamia, across a narrow alley. He and Laodamia see each other through open windows and at Mass. She's almost as devout as he is. Sometimes, when she is walking back from Communion with her lids lowered and her hands clasped in contemplation, her glance darts up to find his. Their gaze locks. Sometimes, after a service, he rushes back to watch from the window as she arrives home and stands on these very steps that he is standing on now.

After today their families will meet. There will be visits, chaperones, rooms of silent aunties and announcements, and the families will attend Mass together on feast days. This will go on until they are old enough and Girolamo is a qualified doctor. Then a ceremony. Then a home and life and a wedding bed. They are from similar houses, similar backgrounds. It's a good match.

Giro's grandfather, Dr Michele Savonarola, was court

physician to the ruling family in Ferrara. Michele didn't like his only son, Niccolò, and favoured his grandson Girolamo instead. Michele took him to his side and tutored the small, intense boy. He could see that he was special, clever, better than the others and destined for greatness. Michele was a professor in two universities and published books on topics as diverse as midwifery and history. He was a public intellectual, a polymath. He was exactly what we now think of as a Renaissance man, but he rejected all this new thinking, was fervently anti-humanist and anti-classicist. He told Girolamo to trust the word of the Bible over the Church, believe his faith over the evidence of his eyes.

Michele died four years ago and left his fortune to Girolamo's father. He was right about Niccolò, who is neither special nor clever. He tries to invest the inheritance, even dabbles in usury, which is a mortal sin, but he doesn't get security for the loans and loses all of it. He's a disappointment.

Girolamo's mother is a Mantuan aristocrat who married for money. She's counting on Giro to save them from penury: what little money they have left will be spent on Girolamo's education so that he can be a doctor like Michele. He will open doors for the rest of them.

Precarious status is just one of the things Girolamo has in common with Laodamia. She is the daughter of a rich family perpetually on the brink of disgrace. The Strozzis are bankers, usurers – activities for the desperate, looking to get rich quick. The Strozzis were rivals with the Medici family back in Florence but lost a power struggle and were exiled to Ferrara. But this is not the worst of Laodamia's shames. She's illegitimate, a stain on her soul that she cannot shake off with prayer or devotions. Everyone knows. She's shunned by many as a walking embodiment of sin.

But Girolamo doesn't care. He can overlook the sin to see the girl. He loves her.

From inside the villa footsteps are coming towards him. The insert door opens, a small tradesman's door cut into the large formal door. A matron he has never seen before stands there. She's wearing an apron with a stain on the hem, has an old, puckered burn scar across her forehead and white hairs on her chin. He has made it clear what he is calling for, as a suitor for Laodamia Strozzi's hand. So, it would be more proper for the full door to be opened and for him to be greeted by a prominent member of the family.

Savonarola is a little bit confused by this breach of protocol, but the Strozzis are not from here. Customs are different in Florence. Or perhaps plague has touched the family, and everyone is ill, but they're letting him in because they don't want to draw attention. Then another more melancholy possibility occurs to him: the Strozzis despise this illegitimate daughter. A high-ranking family member will not be sent to welcome her suitor. Laodamia will not be treated as shop-soiled in their house, he resolves. He will not allow this.

The matron looks at his prominent nose, has been told that the person calling has this nose, is using it to identify him. Her eyes flick left. She knows he's come from the Savonarola family home next door.

He's alert for signs of fever, smells for sage – a sure sign that a house is suffering – but he sees nothing.

She stands back to let him in. Girolamo steps into the hall.

The matron nods him to a wooden bench, turns her back on him and walks away. Girolamo sits dutifully, setting his gift on his knees. He has brought a small present of silk ribbon in a green box. He chose something modest, to show that he's not materialistic, but Laodamia will know that. As an illegitimate girl her dowry is very minor. He wants her to know that he doesn't care. His mind is on more important things. He loves her.

He is left waiting, listening and sniffing, still looking for signs of illness in the house: piles of bloody sick sheets, shuttered rooms. The hallway is tall and narrow, a room that servants pass through on their way to other rooms, but straight ahead is an open arch to the central courtyard and three balconies, one above the other. It's quiet in the open courtyard, but nothing makes him think they're ill. From the kitchens on the top floor a sweet, soft smell of roasting onion filters down. Life is going on.

It isn't plague, he's sure. It doesn't mean that. Laodamia deserves better than this. This should be a joyful day.

He commits the sights and sensations to memory as he drums his toes inside his shoes. This is a special day. They'll tell their grandchildren about today.

Through the wall next to him he hears steps, leather-soled shoes on a tiled floor. Servants wear felted shoes to keep the place peaceful, but the wearer of these shoes is happy to fill the house with noise. A householder. He hears them on his left, passing, he thinks, from room to room until they stop beyond closed double doors next to him. A pause. Someone whispers. A woman. Urgent orders. A reproach. Someone whispers an apology and then the doors open.

A young maid appears in the doorway, bows to Savonarola and motions to him to come into the room. He stands up, experiencing the moment through several time frames: from the distant future as a wistful old man, from the present as an ardent lover, from two minutes from now when it is over. This is the moment just before he spoke to Laodamia for the very first time. Laodamia, his wife of so many years. Girolamo takes a step towards his fate, holding the gift out in front of him as he follows the maid through the door.

Laodamia is sitting in a large chair in the middle of a huge white room, her hands on the rests, fingers ringless, wrists covered. She wears grey, trimmed with red; not too showy, which he likes.

This is the first time he has looked straight at her. Her eyes are green and lined with blonde lashes. Her eyebrows are so pale they're hardly visible. Her nose is an arrow, her lips a russet bud. She may have been biting them to make them more alluring. He has heard of girls doing that.

The tall woman serving as chaperone is a relative but not a prominent one. She stands behind Laodamia's chair, her hand touching her blessed shoulder as if it is nothing. Laodamia holds her knees together, ankles together, eyes down. A small smile plays on her lips.

She is extraordinarily symmetrical. She is order.

He tells them what they know already: his name, his lineage, that he lives next door and is a student at the university, will be studying to be a physician like his grandfather, Dr Michele Savonarola, who served the House of Este and was a professor at Padua and Ferrara. He explains that he has brought Laodamia this modest gift. He steps forward and offers the box to her. She looks at it appreciatively, at him, and then turns her cheek to her chaperone to ask if she should take it. The chaperone steps forward, takes the box on her behalf and steps away.

What does that mean? Will she give it to Laodamia later? Is he talking too much? Should they speak now? He doesn't know.

Giro takes a breath and delivers the eloquent speech he has been practising: I have watched you, Miss Laodamia, at Mass. I know you are devout and a daily Communicant. I have inquired about you and your reputation, and I am impressed. I will one day be a famous doctor. I hope you will find this agreeable: I am proposing a union, a future marriage and, with your permission, will begin our courtship.

He finishes. He thinks it went quite well and he's glad it's over. He was nervous.

Laodamia clears her throat. She settles her feet flat on the floor, the tips of her silver slippers peeking out from under the heavy red hem.

'Girolamo Savonarola, I have been told that you were asking about me and my attendance at Mass. But there is something you do not know . . .'

Her voice is higher than he expected, mellifluous, soft and girlish, the accent pure Tuscan, though she was raised right here in Ferrara where the accent is more guttural. She stops, seems to smile and, looking down, leans forward just a little, squeezing the armrests of the chair.

'To me, you are nothing,' she says. 'You are not of my class. Your father is a feckless idiot. You have no money, and I would never stoop to marry you. I find you ridiculous.'

That's not what she says. No girl would say these things; girls, especially young girls, need to believe that they are good people. But this is what he hears her say. This is what he tells his biographer she said.

They all look at him, the maid, the chaperone, the girl. They're laughing at him.

He burns.

Shaking, Savonarola blurts out that she is a bastard

and no one else would want her. He was doing her a favour. He felt sorry for her.

Then he leaves, tripping over a flagstone in the hall. He turns the handle on the insert and pushes at the full door. It will not open. He can't get out. He's almost crying. He bangs the door with a weak fist. The hairy-chinned matron with the scar hears him banging frantically and comes to help him get out. As he steps into the street her hot hand slides across his shoulder, and she mutters that she's sorry for what just happened. The creature pities him.

He runs home.

Failure had never occurred to him. He's Girolamo. He is the stand-out. He can't take it in. She's a bastard from a family of usurers. He runs upstairs and hides in a room on the far side of the house, away from her, in a room with no windows. He stands in the dark, panting and sweating and trying to stop crying.

He can't accept it. He can't. He'd crash the moon into the earth before he accepts this.

Later, Savonarola will deny ever being attracted to anyone. The temptations of the flesh have never touched him. God has spared him the need for love. He does admit to being beguiled by Laodamia, but only briefly and because his older brother blurted it out to his first biographer. He said Girolamo mooned around after her, watched her through the window and tried to serenade her with his lute; that he proposed and how he was never, ever the same after she rejected him. Later, after his brother dies, Savonarola denies it happened.

His family notice the weight loss, sleeplessness and profound melancholia. They notice that he turns left now when he goes out, to avoid crossing in front of the Strozzi villa. He walks the long way to university classes. He attends Mass at different times and becomes obsessed with the Church, with corruption in the Church, what needs to change in the Church.

His mother is worried. Girolamo is their only prospect now, their long-term proposition. Without him, they will end up destitute. If his mother knew what was said in the next-door villa, she'd start a feud with the Strozzis, obsess about them and spread gossip and rumours, nasty stories, wishing them ill. So he tells no one.

Girolamo turns to a common vent for foiled grandiosity: poetry.

His themes are dark. Sadness. Despair. Disgust at the obvious corruption of the Church. Everyone can see it, but no one speaks out. Everyone is afraid. The Vatican sells redemption and positions and is full of sodomites. He's got a thing about sodomites. He writes of his disgust at the open corruption and wickedness played out in front of everyone.

Happy are those who by rapine live, he writes.

Teenage angst is hardly unique to 1470. Girolamo might have fallen in love with someone else, gotten over it eventually, but for the civil war.

Even for Italy, the brutality in Ferrara is shocking.

III

THE SOUND OF
WALNUTS ROLLING
OVER COBBLES

Ferrara, 1471

The ruling Duke of Ferrara is dying, either he was poisoned or he drank and ate himself into a coma. Regardless, he is going to die, and he's unmarried, childless and with no clear plan of succession. There are two contenders for the dukedom, and both are members of his family. There isn't much between them, but before the duke is even buried civil war breaks out in heart of the city.

Ferrara is rich, the dukedom is very lucrative, and the Balkanised nature of Italy – made up of hostile city states and independent republics – makes each succession dispute a proxy war for a hundred other petty grievances. In this conflict, one side is backed by Venice, and the other is supported and funded by Milan and Mantua. It's the Vietnam War taking place in Monte Carlo.

Anyone able to flees the city. The Savonarolas board themselves up in their villa and wait. Giro's grandfather, the doctor, has been dead for five years. They're not important enough to take a side or have a stake in the outcome, but they are rich enough to be killed just for being there. Their house is on a main road leading to the ducal palazzo, meaning they can see everything.

Watching through the boarded-up windows, afraid to light a candle or make a noise, Savonarola witnesses a purge.

He sees prominent noblewomen dragged from their villas and stripped naked in the street, gang-raped by thugs and murdered, their defiled corpses left in the street.

He hears barricaded houses being broken into and watches as a family is forced up onto their roof, beaten and battered and pushed off then hacked to death by men waiting in the street below.

Across the road a family that the Savonarolas know well have also boarded up their house. No one moves inside. Everyone thinks they've left until, early on a quiet evening, armed men gather outside and set fire to the house. The shutters open on a first-floor window and black smoke billows out. The family have been hiding in there all along, all of them. Four generations. The father of the family appears through the smoke. He's frantic, blackened and panicked. He drops something into the street and disappears back into the house.

Savonarola stands on tiptoes to see what he threw out. A bundle. Yellow wool. A blanket. It was the baby. He threw the baby out of the window. A red bloom grows around the shawl, fast, dark. The armed men who started the fire recoil from it. The baby is dead, but the father doesn't notice. He's back at the window with a screaming toddler. He throws that child out of the window too, and it lands on its side, next to the dead baby. The father disappears back into the thickening smoke. The toddler gets up, holding the arm it landed on, tips its head back and lets out an unearthly scream. Something big cracks inside the house, a beam, and a window shutter drops off and lands in the street. Flames burst from inside the house, but the father is back at the window with a bigger child, a boy, fighting him. The father wrestles his legs out of the window before dropping him into the street.

The boy lands on all fours. He freezes, afraid to even look up.

Armed men gather around him. Other men surround the screaming toddler. Someone says something. A straggler, a young man, picks up the bloodied yellow blanket and holds it over his head. Then he throws it high, straight into the flames at the window.

The men cheer. One of them laughs loud and hard. The crying toddler is flying, thrown like a bag of flour, straight up and high and into the wall of flames. The men turn to the boy, still on all fours, frozen, staring at the ground. The young man grins and takes a step towards him.

Girolamo can't watch any more. He falls to his haunches and stares at the floor.

How can God let this happen?

★ ★ ★

The civil war ends. The city declares a new ruler and honours are bestowed on his supporters.

Peace falls as suddenly as a scene-change backdrop but no one is ever the same.

The afterwards is almost worse because the winners are vengeful and fearless, knowing there will be no retribution for anything they do.

A few days later Girolamo's family take down the boards over their windows and doors, but they're still afraid to leave the house. A strange mood permeates the city. People passing by the house look scared and shocked: they walk quickly, elbows tight to their sides, eyes wide and dead ahead. There's a strange smell wafting around the town, coming from the ducal piazza. It's sour meat and death, a heavy, oily smell that envelops the house when the breeze comes their way. Something has happened. They don't know what.

Giro hasn't been out for a week. It's seven in the morning and he decides to make a break for the university. He needs to see the college noticeboard, needs to know the deadlines for his essays.

He slips out of a side door and listens. The street is quiet. He sets off, cuts past the alley between his house and the Strozzis', passes their front door. Undisturbed soot from the fire across the road is banked up on their front steps. The Strozzis have left.

He keeps his head down and hurries along the road towards the ducal palazzo, but a man and woman block his way. They are not a couple, this pair, they don't fit together. He is a well-dressed young man and she is an older woman, poor. They seem like strangers, but they are standing right in the middle of the narrow passageway to the piazza and they're holding each other up. The woman has dropped a big basket of walnuts. They've tumbled into the road, rolling down into the gutter. She doesn't care. She's standing with her mouth open, looking ahead, the man's arm around her, supporting her as she struggles to breathe. They're looking into the piazza, looking at something. Giro sidles around them. Then he sees it.

He stops. He blinks. His eyes dry. It makes no sense.

Red drips down yellow walls. Bright morning sunshine. He blinks again. Under the eaves of the ducal palazzo, high up above the piazza, a garland of torn flesh. Arms, legs, bits of faces, high on the yellow wall in the bright and hopeful morning.

The victors have dismembered two hundred of their opponents, mostly the high-born and the titled, and nailed them up for all to see. A disaster of war. This is what power does. This is what conflict looks like.

How can God allow this? How can faith combat this?

Returning home, Savonarola does not take the long way around. He walks straight past her door. He isn't afraid of being laughed at any more. He doesn't care.

His depression deepens until neither he nor his family and friends can remember when he was different. This is just what Giro is like.

Lugubrious.

Taciturn.

Intense.

Monosyllabic.

He's a melancholy student. He conflates negativity and authenticity, sees flaws everywhere. He obsesses about corruption in the Church and the Vatican, writes poems about simony, the selling of positions in the Church, the selling of pardons and indulgences for cash, patronage and nepotism, sexual crimes and gluttony. A pope who, it is rumoured, was a pirate once. Everyone is watching this, and no one is doing anything about it. How can faith and preaching the Gospel combat this world? What tools has God given them to fight this battle?

He hates medical school, can't stand to touch flesh or look at it, but he has to do it. His family are counting on him. The world is not supposed to be like this. God cannot mean for it to be like this.

He starts fasting, self-harming for Jesus, denies himself food for days on end to have some sense of control over the chaos in his head. He starts walking incredible distances for the rhythm of it and for the exhaustion that lets him sleep on the roadside and in fields. He gets to be alone. No one likes walking with him because he walks too far too quickly and won't compromise. If a companion gets hurt, he won't stop for them. Bleeding feet feel like a sensory expression of his emotional state. He offers up his swollen knees and ravaged feet as an emulation of Christ's suffering, but it's still not enough.

His desperation reaches ever new lows, and this is when God first gets in touch.

IV

DEUS, LITERALLY,
EX MACHINA

The City of Faenza, May Holiday, 1474

It's the May holiday, and Giro walks forty miles to
Faenza alone. Both feet are bleeding. A toenail has
come off and a blister on his left heel has burst, the flap
of skin drying hard because of the dust from the road,
and it digs into the soft new skin below. The red oval
underneath is bleeding and making his sole slippery.
It's all he can think about, and that's a relief to him. He
walks into the town looking for somewhere to sit down
and examine the damage.

It's past two in the afternoon and the town's holiday
fair is winding down. It's a debauched carnival, with
drunks and gambling and lewd goings-on. A stall-
holder is selling roasted spoiled meat, heavily peppered
to disguise the taste, and hungry children eye the
drunken spit-man hopefully. Giro walks past, expecting
a mouth-watering smell of cooked pork, but it's a sour
odour that hits his nose. A song erupts from a tavern.

At the mouth of an alley a drunk peasant is tit-feeding her baby in front of a couple fucking against a wall. Everyone is unashamed.

Giro slips into a side street, then into the shadows of an alley. He sees a cool dark doorway and knows what it is. He slides in. It's a church. Mass has already started. He kneels down at the back, his knees grinding on the wooden kneeler.

Please, God, I'm doing my best. I'm so trapped. Please tell me what to do. Please, God.

A prayer for guidance is so often a prayer of desperation.

The priest is doing a reading, muttering, voice low, words indistinct. Giro shuts his tired eyes and listens carefully.

The reading is Genesis 12. God tells Abram to leave his father's house, walk away from his family and go wherever God guides him. Have faith. Take the leap then you will found a great nation. Your name will be a blessing.

> *And I will bless those who bless you,*
> *and him who curses you, I will curse.*

Giro, God is saying, get the fuck out of there. Walk. I will guide you, and I will curse those who curse you.

Savonarola starts crying. Hot tears spill from his closed eyes, drip from his nose, splash onto his dusty, bleeding feet. God is talking straight to him.

Later he will give rational reasons for his deduction, how apposite the reading is, how unlikely that he would arrive here in time to hear it, just after posing that very specific question, but that's not really what convinces him.

The truth is, he just knows. Deeply. He knows this is God speaking directly to him.

And God is not asking him to do an easy thing. The stakes are high for his family. Their futures depend on him. Everyone needs him to stay and compromise until he himself is as corrupt and soiled and sinful as the rest of them. God is saying, don't do that.

He fights it for a year.

Then one day, telling no one, he gets up before dawn and leaves. Buddha did the same to his family, just got up and went.

Savonarola walks to Bologna and the Dominican monastery and asks to be admitted as a novice.

He requests the lowest tasks in the kitchen: cleaning, laundry, jobs so thankless and hard that they're usually done by women. He will never be happier or more at peace with himself than he is in this period of his life, when his days are given up to being of service and he is of no importance. It takes him a month to even write and tell his family where he is. He has been aware of his vocational calling for a while, he writes, and was moved to do this by the unspeakable wickedness of the people of Italy. He doesn't tell them that he will found a great nation. He doesn't warn them that

God will curse anyone who doesn't agree with him, but he knows.

The story could end here, with Girolamo finding his place, accepting obscurity and completely absent from the great narrative sweep of history. He could embrace the quiet life of a friar and die with none of his teenage resentments confronted or resolved, no Reformation or martyrs or Huguenot massacres or Calvinist revolutions or Puritans sailing to America seeking religious freedom.

But it doesn't end there.

This is just the beginning of his story.

Because he is still listening to messages from God. And God is guiding Giro's eye to a bunch of stuff no one else seems to have noticed.

V

GOD DIRECTS HIS CHOSEN SERVANT TO STORM THE CONFERENCE CIRCUIT

Bologna, 1474

Girolamo's superiors in the Dominican order get the measure of him immediately. Their mission is to spread faith through preaching, but for the first seven years of his priesthood he is kept away from the public. This is not what normally happens in the Dominicans. New friars with charisma and promise are sent out to sermonise and inspire, to gather followers and donations before the shine goes off them. Although he is an intellectual with two and a half degrees and a lot to say, Savonarola is kept backstage, teaching doctrine to novitiates. After all, he's a favourite with the young. He's passionate and engaging. He makes them feel that what they're doing with their lives is radical and important. The Dominicans feel sure that will wear off as the young move up in the organisation.

At this time preaching is done during Mass, at the sermon. It's a performance. These are not stilted ten-minute monologues about why Christmas isn't just about presents, with fumbled diction and breaths drawn in the middle of sentences to suck the narrative tension out of them. These sermons can last up to three hours and they address all the issues of the day, not just matters of faith. They can be stories or hobby-horse rants, long jokes or parables, because narrative is the most effective way for humans to pass on information. It's primordial. Sometimes they include impersonations of famous people, or a bit of acting and physical theatre, to get the message across. Catholics are obliged to attend Mass, and most people are Catholic, so the audiences are big.

These sermons are like stand-up comedy and, like stand-up, most of it isn't that funny or entertaining. But when it is good, when it's engaging and heartfelt and has something to say, it really lands. Great preachers are celebrities and draw a crowd. Their best turns of phrase or stories are memorised and repeated endlessly, punchlines stick in people's minds. Savonarola knows this and wants to preach. He feels that, unlike most of the brothers, he has something important to say. That's why he joined the Dominicans. He wants to pass on what God has told him, but no one wants to let him because he's such a misery.

He has a lot of controversial ideas, all of them negative. He's bristling with opinions about what's wrong with the world and the Church. He can spot a mistake ten miles away and seems to relish articulating what everyone else is doing wrong. That's very off-brand for the Dominicans. They're quite jolly.

The Dominican vow of poverty means they have to live solely on the charity of others. Their survival depends on them being popular. They don't really involve themselves in complaining, much less demanding revolutionary reform, and are trusted to mind their business, not to rock the boat too much, and do what the Vatican tells them. Obedience and servility are part of their vows. Soon they will be put in charge of the Spanish Inquisition and will be called the Hounds of God, word play on *Domini canes* but also a recognition that they are enforcers, sidekicks – not challengers. The rich appreciate their support of the status quo and fund them generously. The poor love them because they put on a good show when they preach.

Savonarola's thinking doesn't fit with that: people are stupid, the Vatican is corrupt, the world is wicked, priests ignore their vows of celibacy, embezzle alms and gorge themselves on food and wine. Pope Sixtus is a liar and a sodomite and a thief, a nepotist who sells positions within the Church and spends all the money on buildings and streets and bridges and art. And he's a murderer.

He's not wrong. The pope is a murderer.

At Easter Mass in Florence Cathedral, 1478, the holiest event in the Christian calendar, the newly appointed

Archbishop of Pisa and another priest abandon the sacrament and run into the congregation with daggers drawn from the sleeves of their vestments. Giuliano de' Medici is stabbed nineteen times and bleeds out on the cathedral floor. It's an organised coup against the ruling Medici family. Other conspirators attack Giuliano's brother, Lorenzo, but he's faster on his feet and manages to escape through the sacristy.

This breach of the sanctity of the Mass could only have been done on the order of the pope. It's an astonishingly grubby power grab at the most sacred time of the year.

Pope Sixtus is nothing if not shameless.

But it's the effect on the people of Florence that really horrifies Savonarola. Florence is a centre of intellectual life, an international city of scholars and artists and interesting ideas. It's civilised, rich, and anything is possible there. People dream of going there. But the corrupting impact is instantaneous: immediately a mob executes eighty people, and the archbishop is hanged from a window of the Palazzo della Signoria. Other bodies are left on the steps of their family villas, their rotting heads used as knockers against the doors. Children drag the bodies of conspirators out of the River Arno, flog them and throw them back in.

This is how these things happen. It's power and corruption and the acquiescence of the Church that makes these things possible. God is telling Savonarola to speak out about these things. God is loud and clear.

After the attempted coup, a proxy war is imminent in

Florence against two enemies: Naples and the Vatican States. The Vatican can't be challenged because of its trump card: the pope could excommunicate the entire city, condemning its inhabitants to an eternity in Hell. Forming an alliance with the King of Naples is the only way out, but he's dark meat. He has his enemies executed, embalmed and displayed in his palazzo as a message to anyone who thinks of defying him. Florence is cornered.

But then the threat is resolved in a most unlikely way: Lorenzo de' Medici slips out of Florence in secret and alone. He makes his way to Naples to confront the king, surprising and charming him so utterly that war is averted.

Lorenzo is a diplomat: the sanctity of Mass was breached, his brother murdered in front of him, but he will make peace. He can overcome his personal anger for the greater good.

Savonarola is not about to forgive those who trespass against him. Anger is his engine. He's so angry that he has no option: he writes a poem about it.

> *Saint Peter is overthrown;*
> *Here lust and greed are everywhere.*

And then a dispute breaks out between Savonarola and his superior. Dominicans are not allowed to own property, but his prior wants an exception made so that he can own certain lands. Savonarola protests: they have taken a vow of absolute poverty, there should be no exceptions. It gets heated until suddenly Savonarola gets promoted to master of the novitiates and is transferred from Bologna to the Dominican house in Ferrara. It's where his estranged family live, the one place he doesn't want to go. It's not a promotion, it's a punishment, an attempt to make him shut up, and he knows it.

His biographers will later say that he didn't get the chance to see his family very much at this time because he was terribly busy with work. Anyone who ever had a family may read the situation differently.

The Savonarolas are going through a tough time financially. They've had to sell their house and borrow money from an uncle. But Girolamo avoids them, especially his mother. They don't run into each other or meet at Mass because the prior at Ferrara agrees with his Bolognian prior: Savonarola's talents are better used in a role that is not public-facing. He's kept in the novitiate school, out of sight.

His fury festers. His resentment blisters and grows. He tries fasting and prayer and offering up his pain, but God is showing him all this stuff, giving him insights and hitting him with truths no one else has the guts to point out. If he could just get in front of an audience, just do what his mission so clearly is, then he would be able to sleep, to rest, to think about something else.

He's sent to give a paper at a conference in the town of Reggio. These are fellow Dominicans, not soft, fan-boy novitiates.

He walks there, a hundred kilometres. It takes two days, and all the while he is giving prayers of thanks, running over what he will say, praying for clarity and concision, that he will be heard. It's not an important conference. No one significant or powerful goes there, but it's the first time he will be able to speak to a real audience about what must be done. He prays that he moves them. He prays that they will listen instead of eye-rolling or glazing over, the way his brothers in Ferrara do.

When he arrives and sees who's there, he's dismayed. Brothers arrive on fine horses with luggage and servants. Some friars are fat, God's way of telling on the weak. Some are passive, effeminate, or wearing fine woollen cowls and new sandals. They have soft beds in the cells, and the kitchens are full of donated expensive food. He despairs.

On the day of the conference they gather in the refectory, the biggest room in the chapter house.

So far this morning they have listened to the potted history of an obscure point of doctrine and now the second speaker is up. It's warm. Thickened air carries the smell of lunch, of soup and fresh bread. There are thirty-odd people there, mostly Dominican brothers, some laymen, all sitting on benches that are un-varnished, the jagged wood militating against wriggling or getting comfortable.

Savonarola waits and listens. He's next up. The friar speaking before him is popular and pleasant and likeable.

Giro is none of those things. He's filler, not a headliner.

The speaker drones on about charity. We Dominicans have taken a vow of poverty, he says; who can be trusted to collect charity more than us? But the friar is from Ferrara too, and Savonarola knows that he skims the collection for silver and gambles with it.

The room is dark, the faces of his fellow religious are pleased and sleepy, nodding in agreement at some vacuous point being made about all the good work the Church does. The smug talk finishes, the speaker steps down from the podium and all the brothers get up and congratulate him, pat his arm as he comes past, nod at each other. Half the room leave. They've heard what they want to.

Savonarola gets up. No one is paying attention as he walks up to the lectern. He clutches the sides and looks out at them. He can feel God urging him to say it. God is making him reckless.

He lets them have it.

What you just heard was a pack of lies, he says. Charity is one way the rich avoid paying tax. The poor only exist because the wealthy don't pay their fair share, and many of them are bankers who rip people off. Money-lending is forbidden in the Bible but we allow it; we take money from these people to support our luxurious monasteries and convents. We shouldn't. God sees us doing this and He is angry. All this conflict, all these terrible famines and gang rapes and children being thrown into fires – these things happen because God is so angry. The Church is corrupt and it's up to us to challenge that. Priests and nuns are not celibate. Gambling and fornication and gluttony abound among the religious orders. Look at all the fat men here. Look at them. That is sin.

A chubby monk at the back blushes furiously.

Simony is encouraged by our leaders in the Vatican, says Savonarola. We can't be trusted to collect charity because we're greedy and grasping. As long as we tolerate this corruption, God will punish us. Nor should we suffer Jews among us. Nor sodomites. Nor uppity women.

This is what the Bible says.

This is what we should be preaching.

Yet here we all are, he says, sitting in a lovely chapter house in Reggio, looking forward to a nice lunch, networking and back-slapping each other. We're all liars, and God hates us.

It's the oddest paper given at the conference. Attention-grabbing. No one says these things in public, and the delivery is very intense. Savonarola is red and trembling, visibly angry, and it gets worse and worse as he goes on.

Some friars make their way to the doors. Others stay sitting, watching out of concern. Is that young brother all right? He seems very angry. They're only supposed to be here on a jolly. It's not the place for that.

But there are some in the hall who are enraptured by these brutal truths. Young men, young priests. One of them, Pico della Mirandola, is a nineteen-year-old nobleman, an intellectual and a writer. He will be marked forever by what he has heard. It is beyond brave to say these things and the shock of hearing it imprints these messages in his mind. He will, in the future, write the seminal text of the Renaissance. His *Nine Hundred Theses* will attempt to syncretise all the basic tenets of the known world religions and philosophies and will inspire Martin Luther to write his *Ninety-five Theses*, the text that formally sparks the Reformation.

But this is before that, and, in this moment, in Reggio, on a sleepy afternoon at a works conference, an unknown Dominican priest has said the unsayable.

Mirandola and a few other young people rush up to him at the end, starry-eyed and excited. That was amazing, they say, who are you? Where do you get your ideas from? Do you use a pen or a pencil? Their interest is gloriously affirming, but Savonarola resists the temptation to think they admire him. It's the message they admire and the message is from God.

Later Savonarola sits at lunch and burns with pride. Further down the table a particularly portly friar glares at him over the rim of his wine glass. He didn't have any bread at lunch because of Giro's remarks and he's still hungry; quite drunk too because he didn't have bread to soak the wine up. He's furious. Savonarola doesn't care.

He is eating in silence, as per the rule of their order, when he prays to know if he did the right thing. But he doesn't have to wait for an answer. He knows he did. And he knows he'll do it again if he ever gets the chance to speak to other intellectuals, outside the confines of the Ferrara novitiate college. Whatever it takes from him, however angry he makes his superiors, he commits to his mission. All he needs is a chance. God will lead him, give him that chance. He just knows He will.

Finished eating, he folds his hands on his lap, waiting for the rosary at the end of the meal, when a friar appears in the doorway of the refectory. He is young and dusty from the road. He scans the faces of those present until his eye alights on Savonarola. He approaches.

News from Ferrara. The Venetians have invaded. The city is besieged, and it isn't safe to go back.

Girolamo is ordered to Florence and the Convent of San Marco.

VI

WHEN ALL THE
HOPE IS GONE

Convent of San Marco, Florence, 1482

Savonarola has walked a hundred and fifty kilometres, over high mountains and muddy roads, sleeping in barns and eating berries from the fields. A family of peasants shared their food with him yesterday and he promised to pray for them. He forgot initially, but he has been doing that for the past ten miles. He arrives at the city of Florence and enters through the San Gallo Gate.

He sees so much he could hate – corruption, riches, poverty – and yet he is enchanted.

Florence is full of drunks and courtesans and open sodomite market-places, but it is also a city of beautiful art and architecture. It's the San Francisco of its day: tolerant, vibrant, interesting, well run and ordered. Even the children look fed. It prospers.

Or maybe he's just very tired and excited that he will get the chance, if he's careful, to deliver God's message here to a new audience, to a willing audience, to a clever audience. Savonarola has an undergraduate degree, a masters in divinity and half a medical degree. He misses talking to people who can understand him.

Following directions from the locals, he finds himself standing in the piazza in front of the Convent of San Marco. He has never seen any building so well constructed or appointed. The streets around it are wide and bright. The brick is yellow and new. Across the road a garden gives off the smell of honeysuckle. He thanks God, prays he will be useful and goes in.

Savonarola is right to be impressed. San Marco is state-of-the-art.

The Dominicans were invited into Florence by Cosimo de' Medici and given charge of San Marco, taking it over from an order of shabby hermits who'd let it fall into a bad state of disrepair. Cosimo, the father of Lorenzo and Giuliano, the victims of the 1478 plot, paid for all the renovations. No expense was spared. Cosimo was a banker and evil, but he was also old and dying so the budget for this project reflected a rich man's fear of hell.

The complex has gardens, water features, public spaces, clean kitchens, not one but two lavish libraries furnished with books from various collections. Some were job-lots bought after the Fall of Constantinople in 1453, often manuscripts never available in the West before. It's an international centre of intellectual life and discourse.

Savonarola is made very welcome. The cell he is given

is clean and, yes, during his temporary stay here he will be welcome to use both libraries while he waits for the Venetian siege to end.

God wants him to be here. Girolamo settles in, reads, gives talks to students and, importantly, he keeps a lid on the crazy. He finds it easy because he's not as angry as he used to be, less exasperated, and he feels at home here. Lots of the brothers are educated. They're interested in ideas. They get him. After a few months he's asked to give the sermon during Mass.

He knows his Gospel inside out and mostly sticks to that. He speaks for an hour and half about God's cleansing power, the perfidy of women and the evils of sodomy.

His ideas are interesting, if a little formal. The sermon goes down well. Other friars want to talk to him about it afterwards. Those who aren't there hear about it and ask for a copy of his notes so they can read it at their leisure and engage with the ideas.

He's a visiting scholar so they ask him to take a Lent sermon in Florence Cathedral. This is huge. It's one of the biggest services of the year in the biggest cathedral in Tuscany. It can hold up to thirty thousand. This is the chance he's been praying for.

He prepares rigorously.

Come the day, he climbs the steps into the pulpit and looks out at the throng. Not as many as he had hoped but still very busy. He has never spoken to this many before.

Savonarola takes a breath.

Florence is the new Sodom and God is angry. Why do you tolerate all the open lewdness, men chasing boys, that bar down at the Ponte Vecchio called The Hole? God will send plague and famine and war. If you don't change your ways immediately.

People squint and crane towards him. They can't hear, his projection is wrong and he's too wordy. He speaks louder but they don't care to be threatened by this weird stranger. People begin to slip out of the back door. He shouts. His voice sounds strained and high. A whole row of people slide out of their seats to the side aisle, genuflecting one after the other, bob, bob, bob, and away they go through the tall slit of sunshine at the back of the dim cathedral.

Those left in the pews are waiting it out, he can tell. Some are trying to hear, tilt their heads at him, but others are sneering at his accent. He isn't Tuscan. He sounds like a country bumpkin.

He keeps going but more people leave. It's humiliating.

Near the front a small boy sitting on his mother's knee starts coughing, choking a little, and half the congregation turn to see if he's all right. A coughing child is more compelling than these hard spiritual truths that Savonarola is slamming down in front of them.

You'll all burn in Hell's fire if you don't expel the Jews from your civic affairs.

44

The boy stops coughing. Women catch one another's eyes and smile with relief. They cross themselves. Thank God he's all right. They nod to each other. The mother rubs the boy's back and he slides off her knee and presses his face into her belly. Other children fidget. Attention wanders.

Savonarola is still speaking. He wishes he wasn't, but he can't just stop in the middle. He has wanted this for so long, practised so much, that he can't find a way to bring it to a faster conclusion. He stops looking at them. He can't bear to.

At the end of the hour and a half he's left with a congregation of just twenty-five, mostly women minding their broods, staying on until the end so they don't have to go back to work. They don't even listen half the time; they just slump and smack children and make them sit down.

Savonarola finishes. He shambles down from the pulpit. No one tries to speak to him afterwards. Even the altar boys leave without saying goodbye.

'I couldn't have scared a chicken,' he says later.

He's so humiliated that he vows never to preach in public again. They were right in Bologna and Ferrara. He thought he was being held back but the truth is that he's just bad at this. Talentless.

Grandiosity usually finds a way of explaining away the distance between what is expected and what is reflected. Bad reviews are jealousy or corruption or a conspiracy. But Savonarola's problem isn't with his reception so much as with God. Why give him insight and then deny him the means to deliver it? It's cruel. Savonarola can see but he cannot be heard. He can't preach.

There are very successful preachers in Florence at this time. Fra Mariano da Genazzano, an Augustinian monk, smashes it every time but he never says anything insightful or radical. He leaves social justice to the side and focuses on individual failings: the poor are lazy, sodomites are weak, give to our charity and all will be forgiven. He doesn't challenge the structural issues because he's a close personal friend of Lorenzo de' Medici, the current city autocrat. Lorenzo takes Mariano on holiday with him for months at a time, ostensibly so that they can discuss theology should Lorenzo feels so moved. It's to butter him up, really, a bribe to keep him on side.

★ ★ ★

Savonarola remains at San Marco, but his Dominican superiors are aware that all is not well.

His mood slumps. He can't sleep. He is plagued by signs and revelations, visions. He writes them down but can't do anything with them because he can't preach.

When Pope Sixtus dies, he has a fleeting sense of hope. The Church might right itself. Maybe now things will change. But then Giovanni Battista Cibo is made Innocent VIII. Cibo is famously corrupt, promotes his illegitimate children to high office, sells off Church benefices. One of his first acts is to issue a price list for cardinal positions, bishoprics and murder pardons. He's worse than Sixtus.

Savonarola cries for days. His depression and desperation deepen. How could God bring him so close and then let this happen?

Intrusive thoughts become uncontrollable. In the night, when Dominicans wake to pray at three-thirty, kneeling alone in his dark cell, he asks how he could be shown all these visions of how the world could be – honest, pious, faithful – and then be condemned to live in the world as it is. Revelations wake him up, taunt him as he prays. He is a broken vessel, he is nothing, he is self-aggrandising, deluded, an idiot. He is his father.

This is worse than before the Lent sermon because he had hope then. He had something to work towards. But he blew it and now he has nothing.

Months pass. Summer turns to autumn. He stops going out. He fasts himself to near death, but some of his brothers try to help him. One day one of them invites him on a visit to a convent across town, south of the River Arno. It'll be a change for him. It'll do him good. Please, brother.

They walk through the busy city, cross the river via the stinking corridor of filthy butchers' shops on the Ponte Vecchio and climb a steep street on the other side.

As they walk uphill, his brother talks, keeping Savonarola distracted and moving. He says that his little sister is a novitiate in this convent, but she's only thirteen. He wants to recite the afternoon prayers with her, make sure she's attentive to her devotions and not just pissing about all day.

They get to the gates, knock, and a nun lets them in. Once they're inside, the brother walks away, taking a door into the dark, leaving Savonarola alone. He decides to wait in the cloister, sitting on a bench against the wall.

Quiet falls over the convent, a soft, kind peace.

Inside, the sisters are gathering for the recitation, pans and chores set aside for the prayer. Somewhere beyond the door a murmuration of women's voices rises up. He's so used to hearing men pray; the nuns' high voices sound like children, song-like.

It's warm for the time of year, and the centre of the courtyard is full of blinding white sunlight, tiring to look at. He shuts his eyes but can still feel his face tight against the bright white light.

He tips his head back, resting it on the wall, turning his face upward, hearing the distant high murmur then a collective draw of breath like a backwards sigh. The women's voices launch into the Hail Mary.

Savonarola asks God why he was brought here. He can see it all clearly, but no one will listen. The coming of the Cinquecento, the Seven Signs in the Bible. He can see the visions and symbols when he wakes in the middle of the night, see the whole map of it. It hits him like a slap.

Savonarola sits up so suddenly that the front feet of the bench clatter on the stone floor. The noise ricochets around the cloister, and the women's incantation pauses. His eyes are open, irises straining in the sunlight.

The messages are not a cruel joke. They are from God. He knows they are. He breaks the problem down: he's bad at preaching, but the messages are right. God still wants him to deliver his message. The weakness of the delivery is something Giro can work on. And if God is sending him messages, then that, if you think about it, makes him a prophet.

Being a prophet is dangerous. It means that the Almighty trusts Savonarola more than He trusts the pope. It means God is by-passing the proper authorities and coming straight to him: God as whistle-blower. Claiming to be a prophet is heresy. He could be excommunicated if he says it. And it's perilous because prophets are not appreciated in their own land, they're persecuted. They should be glimpsed from afar or through time because the prophet is likely to seem just like an aggravating local bore if they're too familiar.

From this point on everything has to be very carefully stage-managed.

Savonarola keeps quiet about this staggering revelation, but now he knows, and slowly, surely, his mood begins to lift, a little at first, then more and more as he clarifies the message he is receiving. He is a prophet with a message.

He's still a terrible speaker though. No one wants to hear him, but his Dominican superiors are paying for his upkeep and they have to use him for something. They make him tour the provinces giving dreary sermons in towns no one cares about. Each gig is a one-off. He's bad, but the audiences know he won't be back next week, and they might get a better act then. He never gets asked back.

Savonarola, now a prophet, does what he's told, goes where he's sent.

He walks everywhere, eighty miles north, sixty miles east, always on foot, in his little Dominican sandals, and he does this for six years.

During this time Savonarola hones his delivery, his material and his voice. He gets better. He watches his audiences and sees what they respond to, and he gives them that. Actions, surprises, narrative, empathy, threats, finalés. They like all these things. His projection improves slowly, his diction improves quickly. He affects a Tuscan accent. It makes him sound important and clever.

In the town of Brescia he tells them the Apocalypse is coming: rivers of blood will flow through their streets, women will be raped in the alleyways, families will be burned to death in their homes. He basically describes the civil war he witnessed in Ferrara. This does happen. Many years later Brescia is invaded by the French and all of these atrocities occur just as he said they would. Then they look back and wonder how Savonarola could possibly have known. But war is samey. If Savonarola has prophetic insight, then so does the Geneva Convention. This is what people do to each other in unregulated war.

After six years of bombing in the sticks, Savonarola starts to get asked back.

Word of this roving preacher filters back to Florence and Pico della Mirandola, who remembers him from Reggio. He recommends Savonarola to his friend Lorenzo de' Medici: this guy is hot stuff. Get the prior of San Marco to invite him back here. So Lorenzo does and Savonarola accepts the invitation. He comes back.

Lorenzo has made a terrible mistake. He has invited the man who will usurp the Medicis for control over Florence. The Medicis suffer from crippling congenital gout and Lorenzo the Magnificent is swollen, in pain so constant and intense that he can hardly get dressed any more. But he has too many enemies to be ill. He's hiding his weakness. This uncharacteristic misjudgement may be the result of chronic pain or, more likely, he may assume that his dazzle and charm are bound to work on a small-town preacher.. He doesn't know he's dealing with a prophet.

Newly returned, Savonarola is asked to give a sermon in San Marco again. People are curious. They've heard he's good and they're interested. On the day, the church is packed. He takes Revelations as a starting point and predicts three things: that the corrupt Church will be laid to waste and re-built; that the whole of Italy will be punished with war, famine and plague; that this will all happen quickly and soon. He has seen it in a vision.

Word gets out: he's shocking, you *have* to hear this guy.

He's invited by the prior of San Marco to deliver the Lenten sermons for the following year at the cathedral. Seven years after his greatest humiliation, Savonarola gets a do-over.

He steps up to the pulpit and looks out at eight thousand people. He judges his projection perfectly, does the accent and uses every single trick of oratorical delivery that he has learned.

The poor stay poor, and the rich get richer. And the poor have no political power to do anything about it because our elections are rigged. The Medicis have rigged the voting system and hand-pick the candidates. The poor have no chance. There's no hope. Politicians will never change. Tyrants never change.

And how did they get rich in the first place? Banking, high interest rates, and it's a sin specifically mentioned in the Bible. Let's set up credit unions and lend money at minimal interest. Communally.

The rich don't pay their taxes. They bribe the tax collectors. Why are you, the poor, paying heavy taxes when a rich family has so much money they're having statues covered in gold and parked outside their mansions in the street? They're spending all this money on vanity, debauchery and art that is basically pagan idolatry, paving their own path to Hell. How can it be right that those profiting from your loans are able to pass all the laws that regulate those loans? It's unfair, and God knows it's unfair.

The atmosphere in the cathedral is electric. People are coming *back* into the cathedral this time. They're going to get their friends, crowding in to hear him, because the poor and their allies have never heard a public expression of sympathy for their plight. They're always told it's their own fault, that God wants them to suffer. People start sobbing openly in the cathedral.

And the Jews, they're Christ-killers, but they live openly here. We all know that sodomy is an abomination, but, again, openly practised here. We've all seen boys lining up to sell themselves and living, unashamed, with their corruptors.

It's one of his new oratorical tricks: he couples beguiling insights with an unrelated call to action: taxes are unfair, exile the Jews. Politicians hoard power, attack the gays. Income differentials are widening, women should obey.

There are Seven Signs in the Bible, clear as the nose on your face, that a scourge is coming to cleanse the Church and the whole of Italy. Unless we change our ways, war, famine and plague will be visited upon us as a punishment.

How do I know these things? Because God told me, shows me visions of a future City of God, a city on a hill, a new Florence, a People's Republic with proper electoral representation, a city where God is honoured and men are righteous.

He finishes on a threatening tagline: things are going to change around here. Mark this well, because I am the coming hailstorm. Get out of my way or I'll split your head open.

And he steps down from the pulpit. The sound of sobbing and sniffing and cries of revolutionary fervor fill the cathedral.

They wait for him at the door of the sacristy and cry out when they see him. They follow him home to San Marco, try to touch his hem and wait outside hoping for a glimpse. This underclass will be called the Snivellers, a jibe at them for being so emotional and emotive, but they adopt the name and use it with pride, like the Deplorables. They are his core support.

What Savonarola does next is heart-stoppingly brave.

The government of Florence, the Signoria, have a two-month tenure in office. During that time they are sequestered in the Palazzo della Signoria so that they can legislate without being bribed. It doesn't work, because the Medicis control the nominations. The Signoria's enforced isolation means that they can't attend the Mass in the cathedral, so, by tradition, whoever gives the Lenten sermon there then goes up and delivers the same mass to the Signoria.

Savonarola is warned that he can't, shouldn't, mustn't give the same sermon to them. It will not go down well. He can't go up there and tell them that they are irredeemably corrupt and in the pay of the Medicis. Temper it.

But the people trying to scare him don't know how often Savonarola has bombed. He's not scared of that.

Savonarola is followed to the Palazzo della Signoria by gangs of Sniveller fans, poor, crying, wide-eyed and adoring of this man who actually saw them, saw their lives and objected to the woes and tribulations they have always been told were their own fault. They watch him knock on a small wooden side door of the palazzo. It opens, he steps in and the door shuts after him. They wonder if he'll make it back out. The Signoria are in there but so are the dungeons and the torture chambers.

Groups of women stand crying in the Piazza della Signoria. They wait for Savonarola. They pray for Savonarola. They will dress and bury him if they have to. They love him.

After three hours a guard appears at the door, sticks his head out and looks at the women, nods them over. One woman gives a wail. She thinks they'll be led to his corpse. No, says the guard. He's alive and he's coming out. And no, he didn't change a word of that sermon.

Savonarola appears at the palazzo door and the crowd outside cheer ecstatically, touch his cassock as he comes past. They part to let him through.

Before he has even made it to the far side of the piazza half of Florence knows what he did.

They know a revolution has begun.

VII

THE TEMPTATION
OF GIROLAMO

Florence, 1491

Lorenzo de' Medici, Lorenzo the Magnificent, is the richest and most powerful man in Florence. He runs the city and keeps the peace. He has dealt with radical preachers before. A few years before this a Fra Bernadino, a rabble-rouser, was so violently anti-Semitic that a mob of his followers broke into the home of a prominent Jewish trader and tried to kill him. Lorenzo exiled Bernadino, but it was unpopular and he's keen not to do that again. It made him look weak, and Lorenzo actually is weak now, increasingly ill with the chronic inflammatory condition that will kill him.

So, he tries to befriend Savonarola. He knows that it's harder to denounce a person you've made eye contact with. He respects Savonarola's intelligence, everyone does. He just wants to meet him. This is what Lorenzo does. He's a reconciler and a moderator, charming, a finder of middle ground and commonalities.

Somehow the middle ground always benefits the Medicis, though.

Lorenzo is called 'the Magnificent' because he is flash. He dresses beautifully, has girlfriends and boyfriends, spends freely and showers those around him with gifts. The money he's spending isn't always his own: a lot of it is embezzled. One source is a city scheme set up to pay the dowries of extremely poor girls. No one knows he has stolen this money yet. He's just a showy, rich guy who lives large, commissions a lot of art, writes filthy poetry for the most popular feast of the year: Carnevale.

Lorenzo has heard Savonarola preach. He knows he's good. He knows that Savonarola does not necessarily approve of his powerful, rich family but thinks he lacks information. If he knew more about the complex and precarious position their city state is in, he might put less emphasis on ripping up the status quo. He wants Savonarola to stop talking the city down and prophesying calamity for Florence. Prophesying is blasphemous, and it's only a matter of time before the Vatican hears what he is saying and starts playing factions off against each other. He's putting them all in danger.

Lorenzo is genuinely open to being challenged. He is smart enough not to need a moat of yes-men around him. He is the one who suggested inviting Savonarola to San Marco after all. Lorenzo's a pluralist: he believes in discourse, civics and scholarship. He believes in hearing ideas and testing them out.

In a bid to keep the peace Lorenzo asks his pal Fra Mariano da Genazzano to have a quiet word.

Fra Mariano visits Savonarola at San Marco. They have a friendly chat, brother to brother, about why prophesying catastrophe might have a negative effect on the economy and precarious political balance in the city. Mariano asks the good brother to consider what damage would be done by *not* scaring everyone. Does he know for sure these things are going to happen? Is it for them to know the future? They part on good terms, but a confrontation is inevitable now and everyone knows it.

Ascension Day 1491: to a packed church Mariano takes as his text Jesus telling the disciples that the future is not for them to know. Savonarola is mistaken, says Mariano: no one can predict future famines or wars or the Apocalypse. He's a false prophet. The future is not for us to know. But then Mariano gets dirty: he impersonates Savonarola's silly accent and calls him names. This is hot stuff. There's a crackle of discomfort in the church. It's too rich for the blood of many in the congregation. Then he says Savonarola doesn't know the Bible, that he can't even say a Mass properly.

This is fighting talk.

The cathedral is packed three days later when Savonarola gets up to do his sermon. He goes through the text Mariano chose point by point, proving him wrong. Then he too moves onto a more-in-sorrow-than-in-anger tone and starts just asking questions: at

whose suggestion did he give that sermon? Fra Mariano
paid me a visit the other day, he says, and we parted as
friends. What changed? Is it possible that someone got
to him? In whose interest is it that I stop preaching about
my visions? Just asking questions here, but what would
motivate a priest to stand up in front of everyone and say
such things about a fellow religious? Was there money
involved?

The answers are obvious. People are appalled.

It is so humiliating that Fra Mariano flees Florence
within the day and moves to Rome permanently. Mariano
will stay in Rome and will never stop plotting against the
Dominican who embarrassed him into leaving Florence.
Savonarola has made an enemy with a massive ego and
a long memory.

To cap it all, Savonarola is voted in as prior of San
Marco by the other Dominicans. Now he not only has a
voice, he has power.

Lorenzo tries another tactic.

After Mass, Savonarola tends to spend time in the
San Marco cloisters chatting to friends and students and
visitors. It's not a big space, and Lorenzo starts hanging
out there after Mass too, sitting with friends, hoping
he'll bump into the self-styled prophet and have a chat.
Savonarola abruptly stops going there after Mass. He
doesn't want to meet Lorenzo. He doesn't trust him and
knows he's a seducer, that he is a danger.

Lorenzo tries gifts. Wine and food and fabric are
delivered from his house to San Marco. Reasoning that

they are bribes, just the sort of bribes he is preaching against, Savonarola sends them all straight back to the Medici palazzo, untouched.

Lorenzo tries giving generous alms. Bags of high-value gold coins are deposited in the donation box of San Marco anonymously. Everyone knows who they're from. The donations are usually copper coins, and no one else would be so showy about it.

Savonarola gathers all the gold together and gives it out as alms to the poor, handing beggars single coins that are worth more money than they could expect to handle in a year.

Florence thinks this is funny, witty and a great show of integrity. You give us alms, we hand them out. No skimming. Lorenzo is turning into a joke.

He is also in constant, chronic pain – he can't walk or ride a horse any more – and this may account for the clumsiness of his courting. Savonarola treats him with the pitiless venom of those who know they are absolutely right.

The people of Florence are attending Mass all the time now, joining the cult, being whipped up by his preaching. They're refusing to pay taxes or obey the Signoria, refusing to participate in the endless round of lewd festivals and parties. They're attacking Jews at their market, and the sodomites too, who are now afraid for their lives and can't meet openly the way they used to or walk the street with their boyfriends.

So, Lorenzo tries a final desperate approach. He sends

a delegation of powerful citizens to talk to Savonarola, to get him to tone down the rhetoric.

Savonarola knows what they're coming to say. He agrees to meet them after Mass in a small room off the sacristy in San Marco.

He stands facing the door, his hands clasped in his cassock sleeves. His head is clear, his thoughts are clear. He takes a breath. He asks for strength, opens the door, steps in and shuts it behind him and turns to face them.

The small side room is lined in dark wood, and the bright clothes of the prosperous Florentine influencers are dazzling. They glare at him. Some sit, some stand, all are still. He looks back at the rich, prosperous men in ridiculously elaborate velvet jerkins, balloon trousers, cloaks over one shoulder held fast by three coloured cords. A lot of red, gold and green.

He's alone in a sealed room with a lot of powerful men who hate him. If a Medici heir can be stabbed to death by an archbishop in a packed cathedral, then an annoying Dominican can be killed in a side room, but he is less afraid of the possibilities than they are.

Right, says Savonarola, what is it?

Look, says the red-faced banker they've chosen to speak for them, we need to talk to you about safety. Our collective safety. The safety of the city.

Go on, says Savonarola.

Florence needs everyone to stay calm. The French king, Charles the Affable, has asserted a claim to the throne of Naples. He's rich and he's raising an army. In case you haven't noticed, Florence is directly between France and Naples, and he's about to fight his way to Naples, laying waste to the whole of northern Italy. So, we need everyone to stay calm and prepare to defend the city. The very last thing we need are predictions of cities falling into chaos, or you picking a fight with the Vatican. We need to work together to avoid a disaster at this point, so if you could knock the voice-of-God thing on the head, that would be great. Work with us on this and you can have the run of Florence. You can have status. We'll fund your charities. We'll do whatever you want but help us out here.

Savonarola listens. Then he doubles down.

I speak with the voice of God. These are not metaphors or oratorical tricks. What I prophesied will happen.

It seems like things escalate really quickly.

Abruptly, Savonarola is shouting at these important men, shouting that he has visions and the Apocalypse *is* coming and Florence will fall to famine, war and plague. The Church will be cleansed. Lorenzo the Magnificent will die this year. The pope will die this year. The King of Naples will die but I, Savonarola, I will still be here.

The rich and prominent men leave and tell everyone that Savonarola is unhinged. He's mad with power and prophesying all these mad, very specific deaths of prominent men. Who could know those things? He's never even met the pope or the King of Naples. He's crazy.

But it backfires because, almost immediately, Savonarola's predictions begin to come true.

Lorenzo the Magnificent takes to his bed and turns his face to the wall. He's only forty-three.

On his deathbed he calls for Savonarola to give him the last rites, and Savonarola cannot refuse because Lorenzo will not see another priest or let anyone else hear his confession. If Savonarola doesn't go and the sacrament isn't made, then Lorenzo will burn in Hell for all eternity. It's a high-stakes game of chicken, quite a gamble but very shrewd.

Savonarola goes to him.

They speak alone.

No one knows what happens, no one knows what is said, but Savonarola will never publicly attack the Medicis again. He'll denounce many others, he'll provoke attacks, but he'll never mention Florence's richest family again. Maybe he simply doesn't have to. Lorenzo's heir, Piero the Unfortunate, is an idiot. He's so incompetent that the city will exile him and the family for decades with Savonarola barely participating.

Pope Innocent VIII, he of the published price list to get into Heaven, dies shortly after Lorenzo. He was only sixty but so fat and debauched it was a something of a miracle that he lived that long.

Savonarola experiences another brief moment of hope, trepidatious this time because he doesn't trust the Church to cleanse itself. He knows it will take an outside force and his visions are telling him it will happen. Maybe the worst candidate will help the renewal. A compromise candidate could impede the power of a purge. The worst possible candidate is voted in.

Pope Alexander VI is a Borgia. He brings his children and mistresses to the Vatican, gives them chambers and positions and money. He doesn't like the price-list system, thinks they're under-selling, and holds public auctions for holy positions.

He has heard of Savonarola, all the way over there in Florence. He's well aware of the weakness and the cracks in the government of the only city that can rival Rome for riches and influence. Among his many new appointments he makes Fra Mariano the head of the Augustinian order, meaning Savonarola has a dangerous enemy with the ear of the pope. Savonarola has to be careful. He speaks against the Vatican but only in the vaguest terms: principles not people. He never mentions the incumbent.

Meanwhile, the cult of Savonarola grows in Florence, emotive, radical, and slowly the city begins to change, the mood changes, clothes change and become plain: less jewellery is worn, and people hide their gold. Whispering voices against this new puritanism begin to be raised and point out that his black-hearted prophecies weren't completely right, were they? Yes, he was right about Lorenzo and the pope, but the King of Naples was older than the pope and he isn't dead.

And there's the small matter of the Apocalypse that never came.

Until it does.

VIII

APOCALYPSE THEN

Florence, 1493

It builds slowly: a year of rain washes the crops from the fields and causes a famine. Hungry people gravitate to the city and overcrowding leads to an outbreak of a plague. It's not the Black Death but a burning fever that kills in days. The price of grain rockets. Scary stories circulate about the state of the countryside: a starving man walked ten miles to the city to beg for crumbs. He stood at the city gates and gathered whatever he was given, filling his bindle with poor scraps and peelings, but ate nothing. He left, walked the ten miles back to his home where he found his three children dead. The man ate, took a rope and hanged himself in the barn.

Then the King of Naples dies, and Charles of France raises an army that includes eight thousand Swiss mercenaries, who, as everyone knows, are just the worst, and they invade Italy.

The French rampage across the north, raping and killing everyone, stealing everything, burning what they can't carry. Virtually unopposed, they head straight for Naples. They will have to come through Florence. The city panics and rumours abound: the French are ten miles away, fifty miles away, they've turned back, they're coming tonight. Daughters and wives are sent to convents. Everyone else keeps off the streets.

Savonarola was right. He was right about everything.

Everything and everyone feel uncertain. Except Savonarola. Mass is packed every day now: they're all looking for guidance. His statements are definitive, his sermons full of intoxicating certainty. God has already told him the answers.

The French Army is finally spotted approaching, and Florence braces itself.

Piero the Unfortunate, Lorenzo's heir, tries to repeat his father's move on the King of Naples: he sets off solo to meet France's King Charles. But Piero is not Lorenzo, and Charles is not the mad old King of Naples. Piero promises the French king more money than the city has. Charles says, what a lovely offer, thank you so much. Double it and you have a deal. So, Piero doubles it. He thinks appeasement is the same as charm. It isn't. Add half again, says Charles. Sure, why not, says Piero. And the rest, says Charles.

In the end Piero promises enough to bankrupt the city ten times over. Florence has no option but to disown Piero, and the entire Medici family is run out of Florence, their palazzo is sacked, their artwork stolen or smashed.

Now the city is leaderless with a vicious army headed straight for them.

Florence gathers in the cathedral to hear Savonarola speak. They crowd in, shoulder to shoulder, thirty thousand of them kneeling then standing, heads bent in prayer as they suffer through the Mass and wait for the good bit, the sermon, when Savonarola will tell them what is going to happen and what they need to do.

Savonarola steps up to the pulpit and takes in all the frightened faces looking to him for hope and comfort.

You are doomed, he tells them, and it's your own fault. This is a result of your wickedness and greed. God is punishing you. Charles the Affable is God-sent, the scourge we've been waiting for, a new Cyrus. He will cleanse the Church, get rid of the Borgia pope and lay waste to all the other evil-doers of Italy.

Florence, like an abused romantic partner, hears this difficult news and thinks it must be true. Otherwise, why would he say such dreadful things?

When the city sends just four representatives out to renegotiate with Charles the Affable, Savonarola is an obvious choice.

Savonarola, known for never accepting a cart ride or a loan of a horse, walks out to meet the French king. The other delegates are on horseback, but they have to wait for the friar so they can all arrive together, to make it clear that they're a delegation and not just four random Florentines wandering around in a war zone.

This is what the French king and his army see approaching them: a rich Florentine delegation on horseback, gold and red banners a-fluttering, colours high, but they are all behind a small ferocious Dominican monk with a big nose. The monk is on foot, and they follow him.

It is a delegation of four, but Savonarola is in charge.

He meets the French king and tells him that his campaign has been predicted by the Bible. He is the scourge, of the Seven Signs, and has God's approval for his mission. Savonarola and the city of Florence welcome him. They want to support his important work.

Charles the Affable agrees.

Savonarola tells him that Florence will not try to block his passage across Italy. It is God's will that he continues his campaign and destroys as much as possible.

Charles thinks that's absolutely right.

Savonarola explains that, come the day, Charles will overthrow the Borgia pope and be responsible for turning the Catholic Church back to the pure path. The French will be billeted in the city and made welcome, but he must understand that, unlike the rest of the country, Florence is a City of God now, so he'd be better off not sacking, raping and pillaging or burning the city to a stub, if that works for him.

Charles couldn't agree more. He'll come and he wants a hundred and fifty thousand florins too. Pay to keep the peace in the city. Savonarola says that's up to the city government, not him, he can't promise anything, but the billets, that he can do. Confident he can get the money once he's in there, Charles says that would be lovely.

Unlike much of northern Italy, Florence is not sacked

by the French Army. The soldiers stay in pre-agreed billets, and, for an invading army, they're rather kind to Florence. There's a tussle with the Signoria about money but, after a while, the French Army leave and head south to the kingdom of Naples.

Realistically, Savonarola was only a minor factor in the appeasing of Charles, but not according to Florence. His prophecies have all come true. His counsel was sound. The cult widens even further and attracts middle-class followers. It takes over the city entirely. Michelangelo leaves Florence, alarmed by the movement. Botticelli joins it and becomes an arch Sniveller. He stops painting pagan subjects like his 'Birth of Venus' and turns to religious subject matter. It's half cult, half populist uprising. The movement has a scatter-shot manifesto that the followers can pick and chose from. It has many entry points: some are attracted by justice for the poor, some by the anti-semitism. Some are here for piety, some for bloody vengeance. The only thing that holds these disparate aims together is the will of the strong leader, Fra Girolamo Savonarola.

With support in most quarters, Savonarola lays out his agenda: this can be a City of God, but to avoid famine and plague and future wars, they will have to give themselves over to a rigorous, religious way of living, that's the deal.

They extend the franchise and make it a proper republic. They outlaw all gambling and horse races, bacchanalian festivals and drunken displays. Women

have to cover up their bodies and do what they're told.
Sodomy is outlawed, punishable by death.

Savonarola is in charge.

IX

THE FIRST ORDER OF ANY
REPUBLICAN AGENDA:
THE SPLIT

The Duomo, Florence, Sunday 26 July 1495

Savonarola has done his work, beckoning the Almighty into a Godless city, and now he is going to die. He's going home.

He feels his body fail, the cold shadow creeping over him. When the pope writes and orders him to come to Rome and explain himself, Savonarola knows he will be assassinated if he goes. He writes back. Too late, he says, I can't travel. I'm dying.

He has been fasting and holding vigil so intensely that his skinny little body is racked with sores and spasms. He sees bursts of light in the corners of his eyes. He can feel his heart beating in his throat. He's dying and has reluctantly announced that this will be his last ever sermon. He has to make it count.

As he shuffles across the altar to the pulpit steps, a

congregation of twenty thousand men watch him, breathless, half expecting him to die before he gets there. They're mapping his afflictions, his unsteady gait and hands held out at just such an angle that he can catch himself if he falls. But he makes it up the steps and turns to them, looking out at their hopeful, upturned, adoring faces.

Women are no longer welcome at his services. There's no point in them being here, taking up space, when he has important things to say that don't concern them. So, only men are listening as he orders work to begin on a Great Hall so that the expanded Signoria of the New Republic can be cemented. He issues a series of civic orders, revised practices within the voting system to decentralise control and stop corruption.

Then he tells the men – once again – that God will punish them for their tolerance. This City of God still harbours blasphemers, pagan art, licentiousness, dancing, gambling, loose women, drinking and sodomy, and, unless they can stamp these things out, God will vent his wrath upon Florence for the act of just one sinner, as he did the entire tribe of Israel.

Sodomy, the last sin on that list, is his undoing. For many of those listening, the puritan theocracy is where the tear begins. Then, as now, people are wilfully blind to the flaws in their own populism. But the flaws are there. And the flaw here is cock.

Sodomy is an extremely common form of birth control among heterosexuals, and a sexual preference for many. Pregnant and birthing women die all the time. The children of the ruinously fecund die all the time. Men are bankrupted by enormous broods of children, and their exhausted, frail wives need looking after. But the friar says women must bear twenty children, thirty children, be bred from too young, bear when too old, until God takes them or their insides are hanging out of them or their hearts burst with the strain. Men must seed their wives until they are spent. That's what God wants, says the celibate to the men.

The men nod.

But the men aren't stupid. Some of them like their wives, and some of them like sodomy.

In a revolutionary city riven with opposing factions, where neighbours turn on neighbours and everyone is eyed with suspicion, no one reports anyone else for sodomy in three years. There is only one conviction in all that time. It's of a famous bandit and thief, a man who would have been hanged for those crimes anyway.

Those who are openly homosexual leave the city, moving away to Venice and Rome and other, less puritan, cities. Artists leave because the city is poor now. Art is forbidden and no one is buying any more. The Renaissance began in Medici Florence, but it's Savonarola who broadcasts its artistic seed all across Italy and the rest of Europe.

Savonarola knows that there is opposition to his theocratic control of Florence. He thinks it's from factions like the Greys, who, as their bland name suggests, are undercover, quiet, clandestinely pro-Medici. Anyone voicing dissent is immediately attacked by his followers. He doesn't understand that – as much as most people love belonging and worshipping God and feeling part of a giant, glorious enterprise – theocracy and democracy are always in tension. He can't understand because puritanism and pluralism are not in opposition for the vocationally religious.

Savonarola retires to the country to await death.

While he waits, he writes his *Compendium of Revelations*, detailing his visions. Distorted versions of things he's said keep floating back to him and he wants to set the record straight before he dies. Published on 18 August 1495, it's an instant bestseller. Four editions within four weeks. Within a month he translates it into Latin, and that version is reprinted over and over, copies reaching Paris and Constantinople within the year. With a moral vacuum at the heart of the Church, there is a ready audience for radical alternatives, and they can find his work because the printing press has changed everything.

Savonarola is wrong. He doesn't die. He recovers. But God is still angry because, no matter how much sinners are controlled and harried and admonished, the famine deepens in Florence and outbreaks of plague get worse.

The price of grain skyrockets. In Rome, the Borgia pope loses patience. Piero the Unfortunate raises an army and masses them in Siena. In Florence, in the shadows, dissenters begin to find each other, coalesce into factions with competing agendas and become emboldened. Dead women and children, diseased and starved, are found in the streets.

Florence, City of God, is beset by enemies from without and within.

X

THE BONFIRE OF
THE VANITIES

Piazza della Signoria, Florence
Tuesday 7 February 1497

This is how Savonarola knows that he has lost
Florence: not one of the apartments overlooking
the Piazza della Signoria has a candle flickering inside.
The apartments seem deserted but they're not. There's
nowhere to go any more: the inns are closed and the
gambling dens are all shut. People must be home. In one
room a figure is shifting, watching, looking straight at
him. It's a man, he thinks, a man with his arms crossed.
At this same event last year all the windows were bright;
a lot of them were open for people to watch the march
come in for the big bonfire. Last year was better.

Savonarola is losing the city.

He's standing with his back to the small wooden
door he went through on the day of his first successful
sermon, here in front of a massive eighty-foot-high
bonfire of valuables. It's dark and cold and, from deep

inside his cowl hood, his breath crystallises in front of him.

The Jews and sodomites and the bankers are in hiding, the Medicis are gone. All the righteous anger is still there, but the City of God hasn't gone as well as they'd hoped and they're turning on each other. A lifetime of fault-finding can't be extinguished with a bit of good fortune, and Savonarola finds his critical eye turning towards God's plan. People are still hungry. Plague still ravages certain districts. The opposition are mobilising.

He looks up at the figure in the high window, still standing in the dark, watching. He wills them to light a lamp as a sign from God that it will be all right, that he will win them back. Please, God, send me a sign.

Nothing. God watches down from the dark window.

The darkness and cold seem to be deepening, moment by moment. Savonarola feels the breath being squeezed from his body. He's glad to be hidden so well behind his bodyguards.

One of them, Fra Enrico, is a German monk, twice as tall as Savonarola and very muscled. Sometimes, when they stand next to each other with their cowls up, Savonarola feels like a doll of him. Enrico is good to hide behind. On the other side are three laymen who volunteered to protect him. The threats are so frequent that he can't leave San Marco by himself, for fear of being murdered. Florence is waiting for his downfall.

They are waiting in the cold dark piazza for the March of Purity to arrive so they can start the seven-tiered bonfire, one representing each of the deadly sins. He can hear boys singing all the way across the city, the boy sopranos and altos, more altos than sopranos this year.

In the piazza the giant bonfire is surrounded by troops of true believers, those who are already with them. Many of them are crying, perpetually overwhelmed in Savonarola's presence. They cry a lot, unable or unwilling to control themselves. They grab for him as he comes past. He wants to find it touching but it's annoying. He wishes they would stop it. They're making the cause a ridiculous, emotional, feminised joke.

The figure at the dark window stands still for what seems a long time. Then it moves, looking over to the river, to the light from the torches of the boys as they march towards them. But the figure doesn't light a lamp. Not yet anyway.

The crossed arms make him think of his grandfather Michele – he doesn't know why – and a wave of yearning for the old man washes over him. He'd like a friend, an ally who wasn't an acolyte. All he gets now is suck-ups or opposition. It's exhausting. Savonarola's eyes fill up and he clears his throat, embarrassed. Selfish, self-important. I am a vessel. I am a channel. Savonarola looks up at the window again.

The march comes closer. The lights of the torches flicker up high into the night sky and the marchers' song soars over the terracotta roofs.

Oh, not that one. Oh no.

Happy are those who by rapine live.

They're singing one of his adolescent poems: 'The Ruin of the World'. He was very young when he wrote that. He's not keen on that one and wishes he hadn't let them set it to music. When he hears it sung or spoken, it hits his ear at an awkward angle. It's too fraught and serious and absolute. It's his voice but a young him, a man who knows nothing about the tawdry compromises that make up a life. Maybe that's why the boys like it so much. The absolute values and the condemnation of the world.

It feels sometimes as if all of his teenage ambitions have been made manifest, but he is so much older and can see the cracks in all of it now, the missteps and the unforeseen consequences. Ridiculous. When he thinks these things, he has to remind himself that none of this was his idea, not really. These are God's ideas.

Or are they?

The awful song reminds him of Laodamia Strozzi, of home, of the pressure he was under as a young man to do a job he hated and support a family that wouldn't support themselves. Both his parents are dead now. He can't feel compassion for his younger self. He was rich and spoiled and angry. It was all about him. He thought about himself incessantly, his place in the world, what people thought of him. He's seen so much worse since then. He despises himself in hindsight. Even the Girolamo of last year. He loathes the man who believed he wasn't flattered by the march and the fire, didn't take it as a mark of his own importance. Of course he did. Of course he did. Idiot.

Last year was the high point of this revolution. They didn't know it. Then it seemed as if they might set a precedent for theological revolutions all over the Christian world. They had replaced Medici rule with the Republic, a Signoria that represented all of the city . . . apart from the bankers and the Jews and the sodomites and the artists, obviously. They established a *mons pietatis*, a credit union, to give low-interest loans. Jews were afraid to leave their homes after dark, even in the ghetto, as were the perfumed boys and street women. Bankers left the city for Rome and Siena and Venice; that's how they knew they were winning.

But God wasn't appeased: the plague outbreak worsened and the famine deepened. They fed the people by distributing small bags of flour and grain. It worked well until the day a woman was found dead on the cobbles – dead of hunger, they said. But who can know how she died? Women die all the time.

And because they were giving out grain, people from the countryside began to come to the city for food, bringing more plague with them. Children from the countryside were found dead in the street, in doorways, unclaimed children dead of fever and hunger. Death was everywhere. They could hardly bury the bodies. A gravedigger dropped his house keys into a mass grave and died of the stench before they could get him back out.

God was still displeased, and Savonarola knew it was the culture of Florence they had yet to change. Horse racing and beauty, parties, a love of gold and dancing and women and boys. This is why he is here tonight, standing in the cold piazza in front of this bonfire. This is why there is an army of boys in white robes marching around the city. This is why they banned all those other practices. For God.

Savonarola can hear them coming, their sweet singing rising up through the night. It's much too quiet in Florence tonight.

He looks up again at the windows above. The people who live in these rooms are not the rich nor desperately poor. They are the people in the middle, swayable by a hundred variables. But they are the majority and they have elected not to watch this bonfire or participate this year.

Last year they did.

Last year was the first challenge to the Florentine culture of Carnevale. These customs date back to before the Roman Empire. They're ingrained in the fabric of the city, chips on the shin bone of Florence.

In years past, boys would form gangs in their own district and were attacked if they crossed into one another's territories. This is true all year round, but at Carnevale, coinciding with the period just before Lent, the gang wars would intensify. Companies of boys met at the borders of different areas and held pitched battles of stone throwing. Every year some boys were killed or maimed. As part of this territorial assertion, minor differences in identity were played up and exaggerated. Each area set up booths with coloured banners at crossroads, and the boys forced passers-by to give up the smallest coins they had in their pockets. The money collected went towards food and drink for that area's party on the final night of Carnevale.

Gambling and general dissolution were unconfined and shameless during the build-up. The final night was a disgusting display of drunkenness and sexy dancing, a depressing round of filthy songs and poems and lewd public acts. Brothels sprang up all over the city. The sodomites gathered in saloons and drinking dens. It was eagerly anticipated by everyone in Florence – even the Jews in the ghetto enjoyed it, but they had their own customs. It actually coincided with Passover, but a lot of Florentines thought the Jews didn't understand what Carnevale was about and cleaned out their homes for no reason.

Savonarola wasn't surprised that God was angry about it. He was angry too. He didn't see why there had to be a festival at all and wanted to ban it, but his fellow brothers disagreed. Better, they said, to use the customs and change them to praise God and do his bidding. Then at least the boys would be kept busy.

Luckily for them the Dominicans teach the boys their catechism classes. This gave them time to suggest to the youth of Florence that they should raise alms for poor orphans at the tollbooths, rather than for wine. The boys loved this idea. That first year, instead of a threatening pile of stones around the tollbooth to frighten passers-by into paying a party tax, they built little altars with crucifixes and asked humbly for contributions. They raised an astonishing sum of money.

On the final night the boys, aged five to sixteen, formed a battalion of thousands and processed through the whole city, crossing all the districts and the borders between, zig-zagging across the bridges from church to church, gathering even more alms as they marched under the flags of their districts and sang hymns in their beautiful high voices. They made their way to the Piazza della Signoria for a marvellous large bonfire and then onto the Duomo for Mass. The service was so well attended that, although the capacity of the cathedral is thirty thousand, extra seats had to be put in for the boys, banked benches at the side, and they sang hymns that made the adults weep at the purity of the voices. At the end of the evening the alms were counted. It took all night to count all of the coins because they were all copper, small coins, given by the poor for the poor. The money was taken to the orphanage and word went out about the wonderful thing they had all done together.

For weeks afterwards people were emotional at the mention of the service. Truly, this is the work of the Lord, Savonarola thought. Truly, this is a City of God.

Truly, this is the moment when the revolution feels as if it might work, as if it can work.

In hindsight this was the moment just before it turned.

It's different this year, and Savonarola knows it. They're losing the city.

There are good reasons for this. This year the atmosphere is edgy and defiant, no longer innocent. Demands for alms have an insistent, bullying tone.

The boys at the crossroads are empowered and tax more insistently this year. They shake people down instead of humbly asking because, in catechism class, they've been told that they are right, that they are spreading the message of God, that they should be enforcing the puritan message. Some of them take it too far, as boys will. One group rips the comb out of a rich girl's hair. Another forces contributions to the alms pot. One group of boys knock over barrels of wine and run away. If a gambler wants to break up a game, they shout, 'SAVONAROLA'S BOYS!' and everyone scrams. This year the singing is angrier, the banners are higher, the militant boys are older. The five-years-olds stay home.

The city has splintered into battling factions. Some are created in opposition to the Snivellers. The Enraged are a group who hate everything the Savonarolians do, even if it is for their benefit, even if it helps them personally.

The Proud Boys or Bad Companions are rich young men who dress up in fancy clothes and armour, bear swords and hold expensive dinners of imported food and wines. They do so in defiance, a way of signalling that they will not be told what to do. They're bully boys showing off to each other and chest bumping.

The Tepid are the ones behind the dark windows. They are who Savonarola is really scared of. They are the middle people. He used to think the true religious and the fervent were the ones who change the world, but he can see now that fervour is as fleeting as a spark from a flint. The real power, the real history-makers, are the middle. And their lights are off.

All the non-Snivellers share a motto: 'We are for the natural world,' they say. It means they favour provable science, testable facts, not prophecies or blind faith or superstitions.

There's a movement up there in the high room. A shadow shifts. Savonarola's breath stops in front of him. His mouth is open, but he has stopped breathing for just a moment, watching, waiting for a sign. Sudden light hits the corner of his eye, bursting into the piazza and banishing the darkness, but it's not from the window. It's the March of Purity rounding the corner to the narrow Via Vacchereccia.

The high walls on either side amplify their voices and the lights from their torches. The singing is loud and the light floods into the piazza and licks up the walls.

Savonarola sees the figure in the high room is gone, has stepped back into the shadows. God is, somehow, gone. This bonfire and this march, this broad display of piety for an unwatching city, is all a hollow practice.

Savonarola looks to the marchers coming into

the piazza. They're all dressed in white gowns, boys singing loud, ecstatic eyes wide, full of hope and with piety in their hearts. He sees Fra Enrico and the other bodyguards, the row of Dominican brothers, all staring, mouths hanging open, at these happy, singing boys. It's a little uncomfortable.

Row after row they process into the piazza, row after row, filling it up and surrounding the bonfire they've been building for days. They're excited and smiling, a lot of them singing *at* him, and he realises that they're singing another of his poems; this one is about the Vatican and how corrupt it is.

> Saint Peter is overthrown;
> Here lust and greed are everywhere.

He didn't know anyone had set that to music. He hates that poem. It insults the Vatican. They should have asked him. He looks around at his follow brothers, and Fra Domenico grins back at him and nods. Yes, he is behind this. He's delighted about it and expects Savonarola to be too. Savonarola nods back, and Domenico clutches at his heart with joy. He's an emotional person, Domenico, a good man but a little too indulgent.

Savonarola looks away. They keep misunderstanding. He doesn't hate the Vatican. He doesn't even hate Alexander VI, even though the pope treats the Holy See as a personal fiefdom, even though he corrupts it with his bastard children and his mistresses and his simony.

Alexander will not allow a purge against the Jews, and he doesn't just tolerate them, he defends them. And he's wily. He bribed Charles the Affable, whom Savonarola predicted would purge the Vatican, and formed an allegiance with him, letting the French Army pass through the Papal States unmolested. Charles took Naples and then withdrew back to France without affecting any change whatsoever. Now the Vatican is coming for Florence. They can smell the fractures in Florentine resolve.

The boys finish singing the stupid song and a quiet falls over the crowd. The only sounds are feet tramping on stone, boys being ordered about in whispers.

Not that way, Rodrigo.

Tomas, stop it, stop that *right* now.

You've been told – right, you two, move to the back row. I don't care.

Hoi, you, fat boy, *hands!*

A lot of work is going on in the ranks, a lot of shepherding and nudging. Finally, they are all arranged around the fire but standing far enough away for it to be safe to light it.

A hymn is sung as the oldest boys light tapers, one from another. The taper-holders are the oldest boys there. The taper boy closest to Savonarola has a sharp turn in his left eye. He watches the boy, worried his wall eye will make him touch the taper to the wrong thing. He doesn't know what he sees. It's dangerous.

On a given signal they all step forward and hold their

flames to the very bottom of the fire. It is drenched in oil and kindling to make it burn well. The squinting boy does fine.

In the dark and cold piazza, a red line crackles around the bottom of the pyre like a fiery rat running from a cat. The fire is so well set that it remains burning low for a few minutes, giving them all a clear view of the contents.

The first level marks the deadly sin of Lust. The flames catch oil-soaked clay statuettes, copies of the sodomite Donatello's works, the fine bottoms and shapely legs that denote men or women, no one knows which. Books of lascivious poetry are in there too, filth that boys of the neighbourhood were well familiar with and confiscated and offered to the flames. A good job, Fra Enrico told him, because one of their young company had been charging them for the private use of the book and it was the ruination of many. There is a painting in there: Girolamo can see a corner of it. He knows there are several. Three of them are by Botticelli, naked figures of Roman gods. One of the paintings is big and colourful. Botticelli handed them in himself, he and his brother carrying them down. He only paints religious subjects now. He is penniless but righteous.

The fire takes, and the foul smell and crackle of burning hair hits Savonarola's nose. Pride is the second-layer sin in the bonfire. Vanity is born of pride, and this is represented by the wigs and hair extensions that some girls wear. The boys have been confiscating these when they see them in the street. The girls are reluctant to give them up because they are expensive. The burning wigs smells terrible, as if sin is being released into the atmosphere. Hubris comes from the sin of pride. Vainglorious self-aggrandising. Self-seeking.

Savonarola glances up to the high window again but the light from the bonfire ripples yellow across the glass. It's all surface now.

There is a scraping sound and a flaming lump drops onto the stones in front of him. A burning dead cat has rolled out of the fire to his feet. What was that doing in there? Have people been messing about and filling the bonfire up with irrelevant crap? It's supposed to be meaningful, not just random items.

He looks at his bodyguards. One of them is trying not to laugh. One of them *is* laughing, looking away and holding his nose so that he doesn't make any noise.

Savonarola doesn't get the joke. Are cats proud? Lustful? Do they incite lust? Some boys see the dead cat and snicker uncomfortably, some others are upset by it. What are the boys doing with cats?

An escort throws a paper twist of gunpowder into the flames. It cracks and fizzes, drawing everyone's attention away from the burning cat. Someone steps forward and uses the side of his foot to slide it back into the bonfire.

For a fragmentary moment Savonarola sees a bloody yellow blanket thrown high into a window full of flames.

Another song begins. The fire burns high and so fierce that they have to move back. Savonarola wants to go to bed and go to sleep. A friar sidles up to him and tells him how much was donated this year. It's great, he says, half of what they got last year, but that's because things are so much more expensive this year, with the famine and everything, and they really didn't expect anything like that.

Savonarola nods.

The friar slips away, smiling insipidly.

The count is already in. This means the coins were of big denominations, not small coins that take all night to count. It's the middle classes who support them now, not the poor any more.

Savonarola knows then that God hasn't entirely forsaken him – he's not important enough for that – but God has taken a step back just when Savonarola needed him not to do that. He is panicking. All of his careful management is about to fall apart. He doesn't think he can hold it together without the help of God, and God is missing in action.

* * *

After the bonfire, during the round of Lent sermons, Savonorola slips up and, instead of talking in generalities about the Vatican, states clearly that the pope himself is corrupt.

'*He* is cooked,' he says and realises his mistake at once. He rows it back. 'I'm not talking about anyone in particular.'

But it's done. It's the start of the end. His enemies send word to the pope. Guess what he said about you. Of all the men alive in Europe this century, the Borgia pope is the most vindictive, and half the city is against him.

After a round of elections the Enraged take control of the Signoria. It's the democrat's conundrum: if you give them the vote, they might vote you out.

The end is coming.

The pope excommunicates Savonarola and sends notification after notification but the messengers can't get into the city. Excommunicated, Savonarola is not allowed to conduct a Mass, attend Mass or take the sacraments. He can't get into Heaven. Finally, Alexander VI sends a copy of the excommunication order to every single Franciscan chapter house in Tuscany, and they announce it from their pulpits.

You are served.

Savonarola refuses to accept it. He carries on giving Mass and writes to all of the great heads of state in Europe calling for the deposition of the Borgia pope. Everyone ignores it except Alexander VI. He makes it his business to depose the friar.

Savonarola is going to be killed, he knows it. He retreats to San Marco and writes four books in seven months. He knows what's coming.

The Franciscans are the second most powerful religious order in the city. They're calling him a liar and a false prophet. One of them, a Fra Francesco, challenges

Savonarola from the pulpit to a trial by fire. This is an archaic form of dispute resolution: the litigants walk towards each other through a tunnel of flames and God shields the truth-teller. The other one burns to death. Let God show them who is telling the truth.

It's a mad thing to suggest. The last time this was done was four hundred years ago, and the practice lapsed because, every time it was done, everyone burned to death instantly. Fra Domenico is furious at Francesco; he can't stop talking about it. Ignore them, Domenico, says Savonarola, just blank it.

But Fra Francesco continues to taunt him. He does it for a year. Savonarola isn't a prophet. His visions are not from God. Claiming to be a prophet is heretical. The Dominicans obviously had no faith in their leader because they weren't willing to walk into a fire to prove him right.

That's too much for emotional Fra Domenico. He breaks ranks. In the middle of a sermon about something completely different: to just say, can I just say, how wrong it was of Fra Francesco to doubt Savonarola when all of his prophecies have come true so far. Well, apart from the Vatican falling and the end of famine and war and plague if we changed our ways. But these predictions were not time-limited, so no one is getting their money back. Savonarola was right anyway. He was definitely right. Becoming angry, Domenico speaks without restraint. His devotion to Savonarola moves him and he declares that he would be willing to walk through fire.

Yes. He will accept the challenge. Are the Franciscans prepared to do the same? Well, are they?

Very sadly for Fra Domenico, they actually are. A date is set for the trial.

Starved of horse racing and theatre and sights of any kind, and with half the city hating Girolamo and an exhausted Signoria, the bizarre notion of a trial by fire gains traction until the impossible becomes inevitable. It's pretty exciting.

On his knees during the three-thirty a.m. prayers, Savonarola finds himself despairing of God's guidance. He digs back, looking for signs or signals, and finds nothing but ashes. Nothing. No visions. No voice. Until he recalls a May afternoon in Faenza, his bleeding feet and Genesis 12. God promised to curse those who stood against him, and half the city is against him now. The pope is coming for him. The King of France is against him.

He serves Mass that day, in San Marco, and during the sermon he makes his final prediction: Charles the Affable is going to die. But the French king is only twenty-eight and in robust health and, even as the prophecy slips from his lips and booms from wall to sacred wall in the great cathedral, Savonarola wonders if he is really prophesying or just trying to goad God into sending him a sign.

He thinks maybe the last one.

XI

ENCHANTED

UNDERPANTS

Amboise (France) and Florence, Saturday 7 April 1498

It's two o'clock in the afternoon, and Charles the Affable is watching a game of *jeu de paume*. He's a little bit drunk. He doesn't really care for tennis but a lot of people like it and it's something to do. If it wasn't this, they'd have to do something more vigorous, horse riding or looking at things and having opinions. He's quite happy doing this. He's drinking wine. He'll eat in a minute but not just yet.

These are the moments that make up a life. Fragments.

He's sitting at a table with his wife, and she is drinking wine too. The other people with them see something happen in the game and they ooh and ahh. Charles joins in. His wife smiles at him. She knows he doesn't follow it.

Anne is still only twenty-one and terribly nice. She didn't like him at first, which he found rather baffling because everyone else does, but she seems to quite like him now. They have lost six children together, four stillborn and two boys who died, one at a month, one aged three. Shared trauma exposes character. They rather love each other now. Three weeks ago they lost a daughter and he's been frightened for Anne but she looks relaxed today, more at peace than of late.

One of the tennis players loses his footing, his heel skidding on the ground, crossing in front of his other foot, but he still goes for the ball with his paddle bat, still swings a good thump at it.

Suddenly, Charles sees the heavy cork tennis ball getting bigger, swelling, coming straight towards his face, but why doesn't seem immediately obvious, possibly because of the drink. Charles titters and blinks to work out what's going on. Though his eyes are closed, he is aware of everyone around him starting to their feet and a general cry of fright. The ball whistles past his left ear and he feels an interruption in the breeze, then hears the cries of relief around him.

He opens his eyes and smiles at everyone, and they laugh, delighted with him. Even Anne laughs. Even Anne.

★ ★ ★

At the very moment the cork ball passes Charles's left ear, a thousand kilometres away in Florence, two hundred and fifty Dominicans priests are walking through the empty city followed by a mob of Sniveller supporters, down to the Piazza della Signoria so that Fra Domenico can walk into a fire and prove, once and for all, that Savonarola is not full of shit.

Through empty streets, processing two by two, they hear the distant hubbub of a raucous crowd crammed into a small space. Half the city is there. Only men are allowed in the piazza today, and the few figures left in the street, on market stalls, watching children and minding animals, are all female. Women and girls look around vaguely, as if they have unexpectedly inherited the world.

Fra Enrico, the big German, walks at the head of their column holding a brass crucifix high. Behind him, the two rows of friars march in time, their weight swaying left, right, left. They are so singular in their purpose, so of a mind – having just said a Mass that they are certain will be the last some of them ever hear on this plane – that their closeness in this moment will never be surpassed.

Savonarola told them that he wasn't sure the trial by fire would take place today, it wasn't up to them, but if it did then they would definitely win, and that gave them all a great buzz.

He asked his public yesterday during a cathedral Mass, do you believe me? Do you think my prophecies are from God? And they stood and shouted, yes. Yes, we believe.

How much do you believe? Do you believe completely?

We believe completely, they said.

Enough to walk into the flames? Would you burn with me?

They raised up their voices and their faces ran

with tears and they shouted, WE WOULD BURN
WITH YOU.

And he said, because he felt it then, I can perform
miracles, but I don't.

That was a strange moment, when he found himself
saying that. The words fizzed through his body and
then fell from his mouth. It was just like the moment
he prophesied that King Charles would die. So now
everyone is expecting him to perform a miracle, that his
representative will walk through the fire unharmed and
he will smite his enemies, even though he said he doesn't
do those sorts of things. Specifically said that. They're
not just expecting a win but a definitive, spectacular,
miraculous win.

The Dominicans aren't thinking about miracles. It's
the aftermath of whatever happens that worries most of
them. Whatever happens down there, win or lose, the
furious mob will want to tear them limb from limb at
the end. It's a lions' den they are walking into.

There are many different feelings about this in the ranks
of the Dominicans marching but one commonality: they
all know they were manipulated into doing this and that
Fra Domenico is to blame for blurting out an acceptance
to the trial. Domenico is walking at the very back, paired
with Savonarola. He is sobbing.

Someone has given him a scarlet cloak to wear today.
It was made for someone else: it's too long and sweeps
the ground behind him. It must have been donated by
a rich patron because it's glorious red and the velvet is

thick enough to sink your fingernails into.

Red is the colour of martyrs. Domenico justified wearing it on the grounds that he will be seen by everyone in the piazza as he walks up to the flames and walks through them. But the flames will be red. He'll be making himself harder to see, if anything. And the whole reason he's there is that he insists he won't be martyred, that's the whole reason they're here, but he's wearing the colour of martyrs.

It doesn't make any sense.

Domenico is forty but seems simultaneously much older and much younger. He looks old. He looks as if a lot of things have happened to him in his life, that they have chipped away at him. He has very few teeth left and tends to grind his gums together. At the same time, his emotional volubility is that of a much younger man. He can always be roused to a fight: his faith is of the emotional kind rather than a meditative or intellectual sort.

Fra Francisco, the Franciscan who issued the challenge, had a little bit of a breakdown the week before the trial. Someone else had to take his place to preserve the honour of the Franciscan order. An unusually high number of excitable men with martyr complexes seem to have vocations.

The Signoria are afraid of the Vatican, specifically of the city being excommunicated en masse. Since the last round of elections the balance of power lies with the Enraged, but even the Tepid are exhausted with

Savonarola's cult. It needs to come to a head. So, they met last night to bash out the rules of the trial by fire, the consequences, and shut this nonsense down once and for all. Essentially, it comes down to this: a tunnel of fire will be built and lit, one party walks in one side, the other walks in the other. To win, they have to traverse the full length of the tunnel and walk out of the other side. They can't jump off halfway through or anything like that, and whoever is left unimmolated is telling the truth. But the kicker is this: whatever the outcome, Savonarola has to leave Florentine land within four hours. It takes ten hours to walk to the edge of Florence and they know he won't take a horse. Savonarola is done for.

If he isn't beaten to death by the mob in the piazza, he'll be arrested for being on Florentine soil, imprisoned and tortured until he admits whatever they want him to.

They turn a corner to the street leading straight down to the piazza, and the sound of people shouting is a filthy, ragged roar. Savonarola can't see from the back; neither can Domenico, who is blinded by tears.

They approach the entrance to the piazza, and Fra Enrico stops. The brothers stop behind him. Savonarola looks to the front and sees Signoria soldiers guarding the entrance to the piazza. They're not letting anyone else in. The Signoria, controlled by the Enraged, are trying to manage the crowd.

Savonarola's steps falter. He is going to die in there.

He knows he is. Domenico sees him falling out of line and turns to look. Savonarola has to pretend he tripped. He cannot let Domenico get more frightened or he'll fall apart in front of everyone.

They're going to tear them apart in there.

He is having a vision right now: arms, legs, bits of faces, his own cheek and eye coming away in someone's hand, displayed on a wall and being seen by a young man on his way to university on a bright and quiet morning, of walnuts rolling across cobbles to the gutter.

Fra Enrico stamps twice on the ground as a signal to the back of the line. We are going in. Follow me. No one knows where Fra Enrico is from in Germany. He doesn't speak Italian or Latin well enough to tell them where he came from or how he knows how to do all of these things. They think he was a mercenary, but no one really knows.

The soldiers guarding the entrance to the piazza step back to allow them in, holding back the mob who have been gathered there since dawn, refusing entry to the Snivellers who have followed them down from San Marco. There just isn't room in the piazza for any more people. It's busier than any of them have ever seen it. It is crammed. No one has been let in since noon.

Guards have to force the crowd to part to let the Dominicans through. They're to stand in the open loggia.

A partition has been built down the middle, one side for them, one for the Franciscans, keeping them apart in case they start scrapping. A party of two hundred Franciscans are already there. They've been there for a while and stare at the Dominicans as they troop into their half of the open loggia, squaring up, jutting out their chins, looking them up and down like small boys staring down rivals at Carnevale. The Franciscans are being protected by a gang of Proud Boys in silver breast-plates, and their half of the loggia is closest to the palazzo so that, if a riot does break out, they can be ushered inside to safety while the Dominicans are ripped apart.

The Dominicans troop in and turn around to face the piazza. This is when they see the platform. Fra Domenico gasps theatrically.

The walkway of raised earth is thirty feet long and five feet high, to give everyone a good view. Stacked all along the high sides are logs of well-dried wood and kindling sticks, soaked with resin and oil to make it burn fast and hot and even. At either end there are boxes for the litigants to step up.

It looks terrifying.

No less frightening is the crowd crammed into the piazza around the walkway. They have been here since dawn and many are drunk. They are all wearing their loyalties and positions too: the Proud Boys are in full armour and formal attire. The Snivellers mark themselves out with their plain colours and unadorned dress. The Enraged are dressed like people were five years ago, in russets and balloon trousers and coloured hose. They're happy to be here, at what they think is the end of this long nightmare.

Savonarola's eyes rise to the window he watched on the night of the Bonfire of the Vanities. It's open, and a young man and woman are looking out through it, a married couple, sitting on chairs facing each other.

Fra Enrico steps to the front of the Dominicans. Brothers, he says in his heavy German accent, we will now say a short Mass.

They had decided this before they left. If anyone dies today, if they all die, they want to be in a state of grace.

Savonarola is holding a consecrated Eucharist and takes a quick service, serves Communion to all. Several of the soldiers guarding them take the host too. Everyone is very respectful while Mass is on. It gives them all a chance to catch their breath and remember why they're here.

Because of prophecies. Because of God.

* * *

Charles the Affable is drunk now. His brush with danger made him feel slightly hysterical, and he drank more than he meant to and then ate a little too much. It enhanced the day no end.

Charles was born in this château. It's the nicest place he has ever been. He loves it here.

Anne mentions that she might want to go inside soon, and he's sympathetic. It's a hard time in a woman's life, these birthing years, these bearing years. The dauphin died of measles, aged three, while Charles was in Italy on campaign. Anne was just fifteen. It changed everything between them, brought a tenderness. It aged them both.

He says he's happy to leave before the end of the match, if she'd rather? Anne thanks him but says, let's stay just a little longer. A good sign, he thinks. A good and Godly sign.

The game recommences. Others are playing now, not the man who slipped but a young groomsman and another, an aristo. They're taking it seriously. Should be a good game.

★ ★ ★

A message is conveyed to the Dominicans through a soldier standing in front of the loggia. The Franciscans are saying that, before anyone starts talking about walking into any fire, the red velvet cloak is enchanted and you are going to have to take it off.

Savonarola can tell that Domenico is already having second thoughts about the cloak anyway. He doesn't really know why he wore it now, and it sends out mixed messages. He gives it up easily, but this makes the Franciscans suspicious. Why wear such a fancy cloak and then give it up without a fight? Is it misdirection? A distraction from something else he's wearing that's enchanted? Are his underclothes enchanted, perhaps?

The Franciscans had convinced themselves that the Dominicans wouldn't turn up to this, but now that they're here, and so calm, they definitely think something is up.

The soldier suggests that Domenico and the Franciscans' champion go into the palazzo to speak and clarify these matters with the Signoria. Domenico agrees and follows the soldier.

Inside, the Franciscans ask him to strip naked in front of everyone to show that he doesn't have any charms or fire-proofing enchantments about his person. Domenico complies.

The Franciscans then want to examine his genitals because there was a prophecy from another source, an almanac, that a hermaphrodite seer would roam the north of Italy and cause havoc, and they want to check it isn't Domenico. He points out the irony of the Franciscans giving credence to an almanac when the whole reason they're here is they refuse to believe in Savonarola's predictions, many of which have come true.

So, you're saying no?

Actually, Domenico doesn't mind them having a look. What they don't know is that he likes being naked in front of other people. Savonarola knows this, all the brothers do. He's so comfortable with the Franciscans putting one of his feet on a chair and then lifting his bits up with a stick so they can examine them that they start to feel uncomfortable at how happy he is. They make him swap Dominican robes with someone else, in case there are charms sewn into his, and then they take him back outside.

But then there they're worried about him being passed a charm by his fellow Dominicans, so they make him stand on the Franciscans' side of the loggia as negotiations continue.

Domenico makes a counter-demand: he'd like to carry the crucifix Fra Enrico carried from San Marco into the flames with him, if that's okay.

No, absolutely not, the Franciscans say. No way. Savonarola suggests a bit of the consecrated Eucharist. This causes outrage. How can he suggest taking a bit of Christ's flesh into the fire? Of course that won't burn. And if it does burn, what does that mean?

The Franciscans work themselves up so much that they have to go back into the palazzo for a theological exploration of the doctrinal clash between trials by fire and transubstantiation.

The mob are getting restive. It was supposed to start two hours ago and they all got here super early. This is taking forever. Many are drunk, and different groups start shouting at each other. A fist rises above a knot of heads, punching down. A soldier steps over to the fight and pulls someone out by the hair, but the man still looks grateful to be out of there. A surge comes towards the loggia, an absurd cry of *'Palle, palle, palle!'* the Medici rallying call. They're not even here. People are just winding each other up now.

Then a thick fog of the Enraged, furious, red-faced and banding together for strength, start trying to muscle their way around the soldiers to get to Savonarola. Many are brandishing daggers.

Suddenly, one hundred heavily armed men jog straight up to the Dominican side of the loggia, breast-plates clattering off their scabbards. Their leader draws his sword and turns back to address the crowd.

I am Salviati, he declares, leader of these men here. We will protect Fra Savonarola with our lives. Anyone of you who steps over *this* line – he scratches a line across the stones with the edge of his sword, being sure to catch the sun and blind those watching – will find himself impaled on the sword of Marcuccio Salviati!

The Enraged back down.

Negotiations over doctrine continue inside.

* * *

It is coming up to two o'clock now, and Anne is too tired to get up and too tired to stay. She needs a rest. Charles rises and holds his wife's hand as she is helped up to her feet. Anne is just sleepy and weak but she has to let them fuss. It's the job of the queen.

Her clothes are duly straightened, her hair perfected and set for the courtly walk back to the château, and off they go, an affable amble. When they hook arms and try to walk abreast, Charles realises that she is a little drunk too. Just afternoon drunk. Pleasant and silly. He's glad of that because he has been a little bit worried about her, he realises. She giggles.

They talk about the tennis, about the weather, courtly

matters, things that have no consequence, until they reach the steps and walk into the château.

It's pleasantly cool inside, a lovely contrast to the warm afternoon.

This is what Charles is thinking as he steps through a low side door. Because it is a cheering, joyful thought, he smiles and brings his face up and sighs. He doesn't notice there's a step down beyond the doorway and he stumbles, over-corrects and accidentally slams his forehead into the stone lintel over the door.

The impact is so loud that two pigeons on a nearby windowsill take flight.

Everyone rushes over. Charles is a bit dazed from the blow. He huffs and laughs at his foolishness and huffs again. It doesn't feel sore, but he can't see straight. What a silly thing to do.

They sit him down, and Anne clasps a cooling hand over his forehead. After just a moment he sits upright, but the chair they sat him on isn't terribly comfortable, to be honest. He'd really rather . . . And here he breaks off. A vacant look comes over him. A small smile tugs at the side of mouth and he slackens, shuts his eyes and slides elegantly off the chair and onto the floor.

* * *

They have been in the palazzo for forty minutes. Savonarola is on the brink of organising another Mass. They've done several rounds of the rosary to keep their minds busy and the crowd at bay: no matter how angry everyone is, they still wouldn't attack during the rosary.

Messages are being sent back and forth: Domenico has been given permission to take the Eucharist into the fire with him because, although it may be an advantage, it is not a technical sacrilege.

But the crowd are attacking each other. There have been several brawls and someone's been stabbed. A number of men have passed out and had to be carried out on boards. As well as this, the windows of one set of rooms overlooking the piazza have been opened, and a gang of Proud Boys are having a party in there with bawds. Some of them are topless and threatening to put on more of a show.

Through the soldiers, Savonarola sends a message to the Franciscans: can we just get on with this?

The reply comes back: you start, we'll catch up.

Savonarola demurs.

A rumour buzzes around the piazza that Savonarola is refusing to do the trial. He's backing out.

A push from around the corner knocks a man over so violently that he trips and lands, teeth-first, on the logs. He stands up, mouth bloody, spitting broken teeth out like olive pips, and turns to find the man who pushed him.

But he stops, he freezes. The Piazza della Signoria is suddenly completely dark. It's as though a blanket has been thrown over all of them at the very same moment.

Everyone in the piazza stills. Even the sharp smells of men trapped for hours, piss and shit and food and men, even the smells seem to freeze.

And then the rain comes.

★ ★ ★

Charles has been on his back for two hours now, and his eyes are no longer moving behind the lids. They are opening a little but only to white, not showing his irises. Anne has not left his side. Don't move him, she says, because she knows that sometimes an injury can be made worse by moving a person if they have been hurt. She is hoping that her husband will sigh and sit up.

Any minute now.

★ ★ ★

The rain falls like a hail of arrows from a merciless army. It comes straight down. Lightning flashes and thunder crashes, and there's no break in the weight of the rain or the strength of it. It falls straight down onto Piazza della Signoria, straight onto the earthen walkway, washing away the resin and the kindling and the oil, soaking all of the logs.

The Dominicans and Franciscans are under the loggia, nice and dry, but they look out through the curtain of rain and watch everything change.

The Proud Boys and their women shut the windows. The Enraged cower and stand back near the buildings, craning for shelter. The Snivellers stay in the rain and try to shield each other with their cloaks or aprons. But no one leaves.

The rain ends as abruptly as it started. There's a ten-second difference between full pelt and a mild spitting. Then it's over. The clouds part. The sun comes out.

An inch of water sits in the piazza. Everyone looks at the walkway. A heavy log topples and rolls away, and the middle of the earthen mound crumbles like wet sand. Nothing will burn now.

Forty minutes later a representative of the Signoria comes out and announces that the trial is cancelled. The mob are furious. The word goes around that this happened because Savonarola delayed it too long. The Snivellers were expecting a miracle, not this rubbish. They look like idiots now. They can't believe he did this to them.

The Signoria guards order everyone out of the piazza. As people start to leave, their movement makes the water tidal. It washes into the loggia and wets the Dominicans' feet. They are all wearing standard-issue sandals. There's no way of not getting wet, so they shake their feet in it, let it get between their soles and the leather.

Soldiers from the Franciscan side bring Fra Domenico back. He looks ecstatic. He thought he was going to be martyred today.

One guard calls Savonarola to the front and asks him: Frate, we'd like you to wait back until more of the piazza is cleared, if you don't mind? For your own safety.

This is a soldier he hasn't spoken to yet. A nice man.

A man who doesn't seem to hate him or anyone else.

They agree to wait.

So, they stand and watch as the piazza is cleared, and Savonarola realises that the soldier isn't really being kind. They are dismissing several thousand potential assassins into the city and then they are going to send Savonarola and Domenico out into their midst. What the soldier is doing is making sure Savonarola is not murdered in the area that he is responsible for managing.

The Dominicans wait – even this small, supposed kindness taken from them – and then, when everyone else is gone, as the sun sets over the city, they process out of the Piazza della Signoria, walking on wet and squeaking sandals, trooping back to San Marco where they will say another Mass before they eat.

★ ★ ★

Charles the Affable does not wake up or sit up or open his eyes. Despite the injury being minor and leaving barely a bruise on his royal forehead, he dies on the floor in the room with the strange little doorway as his wife sits next to him, hoping every second that he won't.

It takes more than a week for the news to get to Florence but, by then, Savonarola will have confessed in front of the entire Signoria that he was lying all along.

XII

WHO THE FUCK IS
FRA ENRICO?

Florence, Monday 9 April 1498

It's three in the morning when Savonarola steps through the burning doors of San Marco and surrenders to the guards.

Outside he is astonished to see three stone-throwing machines lined up to face the door. The riot was organised and well supported, but he expected that. The street outside has been ripped up for cobbles to throw. A couple of men are lying at the base of a tree, dead or drunk, or dead drunk, but everyone else is watching his arrest and shouting that they hate him. Their faces are contorted. The Proud Boys are there, which is why the Signoria guards have been sent, to stop them ripping him apart. But there are ordinary people here too, some of them bloodied, angry women, mothers of sodomites, Jews perhaps, enemies certainly.

The guards grab Savonarola to tie his arms behind his back and turn him away from the people, turning him to face the altar he has been saying Mass at for fifteen years. Only the gilding shows up in the dark, reflecting the torches on the steps outside. Flashes of disembodied halos sparkle in the dark chapel. It's a mess.

Fra Enrico stood guard in that pulpit with a hand cannon, an arquebus, and waited in the dark for the stone throwers to get in. He held the cannon with one hand, a burning rope in his other, waiting for the mob to break down the doors. When they did, the giant German touched the fuse with the burning rope and the cannon fired at them, killing a man and blowing the rest of them off their feet, blinding a woman and knocking over the pews.

The invaders retreated to the corners, some to the street, and that gave him time to reload. He fired it at them several times.

Savonarola didn't know such a thing as a hand cannon existed. And he didn't know that the brothers had anticipated defending him and built up an armoury in one of the cellar rooms, but no one will believe that. He has been saying that Enrico should surrender for hours. But no one will believe that either.

The trial by fire was two days ago and, by the order of the Signoria, he should be off Florentine land. It took a day and a half for them to come for him, though. Everyone was a little stunned at what happened.

But no one knew what to make of the aborted trial by fire. There were no clear plans for what to do in the event of an act of God making the whole thing impossible. Everyone had been ready for a showdown and the Snivellers told their enemies to expect a dramatic miracle, not a bit of good luck. Savonarola doesn't know Charles is dead yet. No one in Florence does. They're embarrassed and have slid back into the shadows, as if Savonarola let them down. They deny him.

Not everyone does, though. Many of his brothers have offered to surrender with him, but he only agrees to be accompanied by Fra Domenico. Domenico stands next to him now, passive and dignified for once.

The soldiers form a loose cordon around the pair and lead them down the steps to the street. Angry people throw rubbish and stones and reach in for a slap or a punch as they are marched down through the ruined town.

Fires in the streets. Twenty dead in the riots, he'll hear later.

All of the civic resentments of the past five years have been played out tonight.

They get down to the Piazza della Signoria. It is lit with torches on the outside walls, the windows bright. Soldiers surround it, keeping it safe from the rioters, because things could have gone either way. A filthy man manages to slither between two of the soldiers and kicks Savonarola in the backside and shouts that the prophecies were coming from there. Then he laughs and gets shoved out of the way by a soldier with a hand the size of the man's face.

They take him through the small side door, the door

he took when he delivered his first great sermon to the Signoria.

The door shuts behind them and this is when Savonarola remembers what comes next, what strappado is.

XIII

STRAPPADO

Palazzo della Signoria, Florence, Monday 9 April 1498

They have taken Domenico to the basement cells and Savonarola to the high tower, keeping them apart. But they won't lose any time. The men charged with questioning him are brought up in the middle of the night, and he is taken down to the cellar.

Now he is standing chained to a wall, looking at the rack. It's a bed of four rollers that move independently with shackles, two above, two below, to fasten the person onto. It makes a mess of the body, breaks bones and cracks spines. If administered too quickly, it can break a person's neck. He doesn't know what to hope for.

But they're not going to use the rack on him. They don't want marks that show, because Savonarola's public appearances are by no means over.

It'll be strappado.

A hooded executioner arrives before the confession-taker and the minute secretary. They have to wait for them. Savonarola asks for a drink of water and is denied. They continue to wait. The executioner's hood seems to be itchy. He reaches under it and scratches his scalp, rubs his nose. It's hot down here. It smells of sewers. Finally, he pulls it off and shows Savonarola his face, defiant and angry.

They lock eyes. What can I do, Savonarola thinks, why be angry at me? But the executioner is angry. Maybe he's just an angry man.

The sun is coming up outside the high window as Ser Ceccone arrives. He is wearing a clean white shift and a blue velvet robe and has a big belly and a small brass bell that he rings when he wants the next thing to happen.

A chair is set down for him. He sits in it without a word. He looks at the rope hanging from the high ceiling and rings his little bell.

The executioner walks over to the wall and uses a crank to lower the rope down to where he can reach it. He holds onto the hook and goes over to Savonarola. He unchains his feet and drags him under the hoist for the hooked rope. Savonarola's hands are still tied behind his back. The executioner tests the binding around his wrists. It's a little loose. He tuts, takes the ropes off and ties it back on tighter. He attaches the hook to the rope and goes back over to the crank.

They wait for Ser Ceccone. He lets them wait.

The bell rings once, and the executioner turns the crank until the rope tightens on the bindings around Savonarola's wrists, pulling his arms up behind him until he is lifted off his feet.

Slowly, Savonarola is hoisted fifteen feet from the

ground by the rope, his arms straining at the shoulder joints. He is left to dangle there, staring down at the greasy stone slabs as pain floods his body in thrums of red fire.

Ser Coccone makes them wait. He hums to himself. Then he stops.

The sweet tinkle of a little bell.

The scraping sound of a wooden peg coming out of the hole in the crank. It seems to go on for a year. Then Savonarola plummets.

As the torture goes on, as they do this over and over and his shoulders are dislocated and his ribs are cracked, he will come to treasure the plummeting moments. When he is falling, he can't feel anything because adrenaline is flooding his body.

But the falling always ends.

The rope tightens, taut, stiff, and he jerks to a stop five feet from the floor, face down. Blinding white light floods through him, radiating from his shoulders through his head, his chest, his lungs. The pain is so acute that he faints and wakes and faints again. He has emptied himself. Shit runs down his legs into his sandals, drips off his toes. He can hear it spatter onto the stone.

Ser Coccone waits. He rings his little bell.

Savonarola is lowered down. The rope is unhooked. He falls to his side on the stone slabs and thinks of the toddler screaming back in Ferrara. Savonarola can't scream. He can't breathe.

A stocky man, a different man, white shirt sleeves

rolled up, comes over and squeezes Savonarola's shoulders. No, sir, his shoulders aren't dislocated, he tells Ser Coccone.

He's good to go again.

XIV

THE FINAL MIRACLE

Piazza della Signoria, Florence, Wednesday 23 May 1498

Savonarola is about to be executed. It is a month since his public confession. They haven't stopped torturing him since then. He doesn't know what else they want him to say, but he knows they need him dead. The pope is asking for him to be sent to Vatican but they can't let him go. Savonarola has shown that he's not a man who can resist torture. He'll give Alexander VI any information he has: where the city gold is kept, how much there is, who the Florentine spies and friends in the Vatican are. When he signed the confession and stood in front of the council in the Great Hall, he knew that they would have to kill him.

His left arm is completely paralysed now, and he can hardly move the fingers on the right one. He's very thin, as thin as he has ever been, because refusing food is the one bit of control he has now. When his stomach is convulsing with hunger so badly that he can see it through his skin, he looks down and watches and reminds himself that he did that. He made that happen.

Footsteps and the sound of chains rattling come closer. Fra Domenico and Fra Silvestro are brought over to him. They greet each other.

Savonarola didn't know they had Fra Silvestro here. He's an older priest, they were never very close, and he doesn't really know why they picked him up. They came for him three nights later, says Silvestro. He doesn't know why either. He's confused and frightened and has a fever, is drooling from one side of his mouth. He has an open injury on his shoulder. It smells bad and is leaking something that isn't blood onto his garments.

Domenico is beatific. He has lost a lot of weight and the few teeth he had left. He looks a hundred years old, but there is a lightness in his eyes and he seems to be radiating peace, even in this dark corridor lined by large soldiers dressed in black. He rehearsed his own death so often, so completely, prior to the trial by fire that he is as ready to die as anyone will ever be. He has said his confession, had absolution. Savonarola envies him. This is a man going to a good death.

Domenico kept faith in Savonarola's prophecies. He was tortured more than Savonarola, but his faith never faltered. He understands Savonarola, though, knows how hard it is to keep faith with oneself.

'Forgive yourself,' he says. 'Forgive.'

The door is shoved open from outside, the corridor fills with dazzling bright light, and all three of them flinch, not just at the day but at the lack of smell, at the freshness of the air. They have been in here for a month.

The light is harsh and hurtful as they walk out. A hiss rises up from the crowd like a murmuration of starlings, rising as of one, twisting and bending and taking off.

The first face Savonarola sees is the boy with the sharp turn in his left eye, but he's not a boy any more. He's a man, suddenly a grown-up. His face is blank and he's dressed in rags with a jaunty hat pulled down over one ear. A thug hat. He throws a stone at Girolamo, but it bounces off a soldier's arm. The boy-man dodges out of the way and appears again a moment later, deeper into the mob. There are a lot of stone-throwing boys here. They do it as if it's a job, dutifully, heavy with ennui. They're being paid to throw stones, by Proud Boys or someone else. But there are people here whose hate is sincere and personal. They catcall and spit at his feet as the three brothers step out into the day.

They're on a long platform built along the side of the palazzo. There are seats on the platform, all facing out to the gathered crowd, set out in three distinct stations. A bishop presides over the first one. Another bishop sits at the second one. The third has five members of the Signoria at it. Each has a table. The first is an altar covered in a white cloth with three heavy gold crucifixes.

Then he sees it: at the far end of this platform a wooden runway juts out at an angle, leading to a high gibbet over a bonfire of brush and tinder sticks. A large wooden cross. A crucifix. The mob have been shouting objections about this all morning; he has been hearing them as he says his prayers. Too good for a heretic, they were saying, cut down one arm at least. They don't seem to have done anything about it, though.

The brothers stand with their backs to the crowd, listening as they are spoken to, declaimed at, read to by the soldier. There will be three different formal hearings conducted before the execution of the three friars.

The first is conducted by a bishop sent by the Vatican. This man was once a priest in San Marco under Savonarola. He is young and handsome, a dark-haired man with startling blue eyes framed by long black lashes. They used to tease him about his looks, say he was temptation incarnate, and he would blush and not know what to say. He was fifteen and unsure of who he was. Now it is Savonarola who's unsure. He doesn't know whether the bishop asked to be here to conduct Savonarola's execution because he hated him all along, or if he has been sent here as a reliable lackey of the Vatican. He can't read it on his face, either.

The bishop stands up and raises his hands. A document is unscrolled in front of him by a page and held up to his face. He reads aloud the Latin words that strip Savonarola, Domenico and Silvestri of their priesthood. His voice breaks once or twice but his face doesn't move. He won't look at them. He keeps his eyes on the text, as if ashamed of what he's doing.

This ceremony is derived from the treatment of disgraced Roman centurions. They are incanted at, the form of words being an important factor in everything the Church does. The bishop can't look Savonarola in the eye as he says he separates the friars from the Church Militant and the Church Triumphant.

No, Savonarola interrupts him gently, no, bishop, you're wrong. The Church Triumphant comes on the Day of Judgement, when the Church rules all. You may have the authority to expel me from the Church Militant, but I'm afraid that Heaven is not within your jurisdiction. You've made a mistake in the spell.

The bishop still won't look at him but concedes the point, reiterates and then carries on.

Their priestly robes and cassocks are removed until they wear nothing but their wide-sleeved white shifts.

The three friars shuffle along to the next station, where a second tribunal is conducted by another bishop. He has also been sent by the Vatican and has plenary indulgences for all of them from the pope. These absolve them of all their sins and from the need to spend any time in Purgatory. They'll go straight to Heaven. They didn't know that was going to happen. Domenico cries with gratitude.

The next tribunal consists of the representatives of the Signoria. They proclaim them guilty of the charges and declare that they are to be hanged and burned. They then bring out a razor and shave their heads and their hands, as is customary in this type of death.

The three condemned men are led to the gibbet by guards. They stand shivering. They're only wearing their thin shifts, and it's a cold day.

The street boys bray disinterestedly. Across the piazza,

a dog barks and other dogs answer. Someone calls from the crowd to Savonarola to perform a miracle if he can. Get yourself out of this one. They sound half hopeful. People jeer and laugh, but no one looks away. Maybe he will perform a miracle. Maybe now.

The executioner takes Fra Silvestro first. He leads the broken man up the steps of the ladder propped against the gibbet. It's good that he's first because he is the most afraid of the three of them.

Fra Domenico is in a state of grace. He's ready to go home. He looks around as if he is about to announce an astonishing feat of alms-gathering that the parish has achieved, smiling when he catches anyone's eye. He could be waiting to buy tomatoes.

Savonarola is praying furiously, his lips slipping over one another, his eyes shut, his forehead knotted tightly.

They're trying to do it quickly, get it over with. They slip the noose around Silvestro's neck and kick him off the ladder. But they've used too short a rope and the slip-knot doesn't work. His arms fly up in a startle reflex, his legs stiffen, his eyes widen and he slowly turns red as he chokes to death. Jesu, he says, Jesu. He says this several times as his face puffs up, then he mouths it, he starts kicking, an involuntary movement of the lower torso, a reflex again, the body trying to find purchase where there is none. His body twists on the rope and then he shits himself. No one even jeers. It isn't very nice to watch.

Now he's dangling, spinning, as shit drips off his feet

into the unlit fire. The executioner is a bit embarrassed in front of the crowd because everyone knows it was his job to sort the ropes out and he messed it up.

He slides down the ladder, feet on the sides, and takes Fra Domenico's arm. He does so roughly, expecting resistance after the unpleasant display, but Domenico goes willingly. At the top of the ladder Domenico looks worried. But he blinks, and he mutters what looks like a prayer as the noose is fitted over his neck. The executioner runs the slip-knot up the rope on this one, looking puzzled, as if the mistake with the last rope was inexplicable and certainly not in anyway related to his competence.

Then he kicks Domenico off the ladder.

This rope works much better. Domenico get off one 'Jesu' before his tongue swells up and fills his mouth, and then he's dead. Shit drips from his heel.

The executioner looks out over the crowd. He seems a little thrilled at the size of the crowd. He may never stand in front of this many people again and he's enjoying the attention.

He makes a face, a mime of trying to remember what he's supposed to do now, and some shout, 'Chief Sniveller, the Chief Sniveller!'

He slides down again and gets Savonarola.

Savonarola is much smaller than the other two.

The executioner towers over him and drags him to the ladder. Savonarola has trouble balancing on the steps because his knee is collapsing and he can't use his arms.

They're swinging pointlessly, bound behind him but completely flaccid.

He gets there, to the top, and the executioner fits the rope around his neck.

The crowd sees Savonarola mouth something that looks a lot like *te absolvo* to his executioner. The executioner's eyes widen indignantly. He mouths something back, something that looks a lot like *fuck off* and he kicks Savonarola off the ladder so suddenly that he breaks his neck. It kills him instantly.

The crowd cheers wildly, frantically. It's the last chance they'll get. The executioner doesn't want to get down. He looks out at the mob and reaches over, grabs the rope Savonarola is hanging from and yanks it, jerking it around, making the friar dance for those he forbade from dancing. He makes a bitter-sounding snickering laugh, and some people join in. Most don't think it's funny, though. A few people are crying. Even to those who hate him, it feels like a petty waste. Something bigger than a man has died.

A sudden fire erupts from the kindling. Someone in the crowd was so offended by the executioner's crude joke that they've lit the bonfire while he's still up the ladder in the middle of it. He jumps down, pulling his ladder with him. Twists of gunpowder are thrown into the flames and showers of orange sparks fly over the heads in the crowd.

The flames take quickly.

They have hung the three men high on a tall gibbet,

so that they will burn for a long time and give the mob satisfaction. The flames have a long way to go to burn their feet. The fire rises. People watch, open-mouthed.

There isn't going to be a miracle. It's such a waste.

The fire is building. The flames rise, the heat intensifies, and then Savonarola's hand rises up, cupped, as if in benediction.

It rises over the heads of all those present as the flames nibble his feet. Women call out that it's a miracle, blessed be to God, a miracle, he is blessing them all. Proud Boys leave the piazza, pale and shaken. It's perfectly explicable.

People here understand fire in the way that we understand remote controls. They know that, probably, the fire burned through the rope around the friar's wrists, that his arms were withered away to nothing from a month of strappado. His cassock has wide sleeves and his body is up high. The sleeve must have filled up with hot air and rose and the cupped hand contained the air. But then the hot air left the sleeve, slipped through his fingers and his hand dropped back down again. It was not a miracle, it's just very creepy, like so much of Savonarola's story.

The bodies are burning now, melting. The cassock has burned off Domenico, and the hair on his chest and legs is aflame like a red halo of sparkles all around him. They watch for a while. The crowd thins, the agony over.

Domenico's body falls into the flames first. Then Silvestro. Savonarola topples in just afterwards. The executioner and two others throw in resin-soaked logs to heat up the fire and burn up the bodies as much as possible. It takes hours.

Later, the guards break up the fire, use a shovel to smash up whatever bones are left and still smoldering. They shovel what they find into two wheelbarrows and roll them down to the river, flanked by armed soldiers.

The Ponte Vecchio is where the butchers' shops are. It stinks. At this time of day the road surface is slippery with fat and blood.

The soldiers wheel the barrows of ashes and bones right to the very middle of the bridge, to the opening over the fat greedy river. The first barrow is tipped and the still-warm remains billow down, swallowed by the grey water. Children watching from the bank of the Arno cheer and shout. One of the soldiers waves at them. Everyone is smiling. The second barrow moves into place and tips again. A grey cloud of dust falls to the water and a second cheer rises from the banks, fainter this time.

It's over. They're doing this bring it all to a clean end, to stop people taking relics. They don't want his faithful followers to have any remains of Savonarola to worship or pray to and ascribe miracles to.

It's finally over. Everyone can go back to normal. Savonarola will be forgotten.

They think they've won.

XV

THE NEW RELICS

1498–

But they're wrong.

Savonarola doesn't need to leave a corpse or bones. Bones aren't relics any more. The world has moved on.

When the hostility and constant assassination threats forced him to stay in his cell in San Marco, he spent all of those months writing.

He wrote down all of his visions, his social justice programme, the careful theology of his anti-Semitism. He wrote down all of the lectures he used to give on doctrine to his novitiates. He gave interviews about his life to his biographer. He used his notes to write his sermons out in long form and annotated them, backing up his points with Bible passages. He wrote prayers and calls to action. He wrote essays about the things that must not be said: the Vatican is corrupt.

The Bible is the truth.

Trust no one but the book.

The intervention of priests isn't necessary to reach God. God speaks straight to his people.

Anyone can be a prophet.

The Jews and the gays and the women are to blame.

These papers were so incendiary that the Dominican brothers hid them during the siege of San Marco, tucking them behind bookshelves and hiding them in cellars until they could get them off the premises. During Fra Domenico's weeks of torture, he sent orders to get the Frate's papers out of Florence. Smuggle them, he said. Get them to safety.

And so, in bales of hay and baskets of linen, tucked into belts worn under cassocks, sewn into secret pockets of cloaks, the papers are taken from the city and delivered to sympathetic outsiders. They're copied and disseminated, translated into many languages, passed from hand to hand in a human chain that crosses Europe. That Savonarola died for saying these things only adds to their power.

His works are mass produced on hand presses, cheap editions and luxury tomes, until copies are held in all the great libraries of Europe and scholars read them, examine them, discuss them and copy out passages themselves.

Savonarola left relics, but not thigh bones or a miraculously unmouldering corpse. Writing is the new reliquary.

His work will be read by Martin Luther and inspire him in his own work. Luther uses Savonarola's theology and tactics, stating shocking truths, challenging orthodoxies and kicking off the Reformation. This religious conflict will rip Europe apart and cause wars so expensive that colonial exploitation for gain becomes essential. These are the wars and conflicts that propel the Puritans to a continent named after Amerigo Vespucci, a neighbour of Sandro Botticelli.

The oratorical tricks and ticks Savonarola learned during his years in the wilderness are monkied by populists to this day: opposing scientific evidence with faith, strong leaders offering intoxicating absolutes who will not be questioned, who deflect dissent with grim warnings of enemies within and without. Followers will again reject the evidence of their eyes to enjoy the luxury of belonging, ignore the despotism they support in the name of decency and national pride, while warm water laps at their feet, icebergs crash into the sea, journalists are executed and cattle trucks stand idle, doors yawning open, waiting for the gays and the Jews, for the natives, the refugees and the poor, and all the noncompliant women.

Sparks from his fires still burn.

This world is the aftermath of Girolamo Savonarola.

The ear is burning, sounds are burning . . .
and despair.
The nose is burning, odours are burning . . .
and despair.
The tongue is burning, flavours are burning . . .
and despair.
The body is burning, tangibles are burning . . .
and despair.

Buddha's *Fire Sermon*